107

THE FIRST BOOK OF
THE McFLANNELS

THE FIRST BOOK OF
THE
McFLANNELS

HELEN W. PRYDE

THOMAS NELSON AND SONS LTD
LONDON EDINBURGH PARIS MELBOURNE
TORONTO AND NEW YORK

THOMAS NELSON AND SONS LTD

Parkside Works Edinburgh 9
3 Henrietta Street London WC2
312 Flinders Street Melbourne C1
91–93 Wellington Street West   Toronto 1

THOMAS NELSON AND SONS
385 Madison Avenue New York 17

SOCIÉTÉ FRANÇAISE D'ÉDITIONS NELSON
25 rue Henri Barbusse Paris V^e

———

First published 1947

FOREWORD

To commend the McFlannels to their friends is unnecessary : to their enemies, unavailing. Mrs. Pryde's characters speak for themselves in their honest, pungent, racy, homely idiom. I offer only one observation and make an acknowledgement. Scottish Broadcasting has gladly enriched itself from the comic figures of Scottish prose writing : Wee Macgregor, Christina, Erchie my Droll Freend, Para Handy, Mansie Waugh, and so back to Bailie Nicol Jarvie ; in these pages we see the process reversed in the spirit of lease-lend, and for the first time broadcasting gives a set of air-born characters to readers. Very many of them will need no introduction for the McFlannels have a million friends who take weekly account of their doings on the Scottish Home Service, and who will be glad to have them preserved on the pages of a new kind of Family Album. Readers meeting the McFlannels for the first time will recognize a new tributary to a familiar stream of Scottish humour, although, typifying so much of our twentieth-century Scotland, they are industrialized townsfolk.

The McFlannel house may be a room and kitchen up a tenement close, but this book about them is a treasure house of good humour, good observation, and good sense.

ANDREW STEWART
Scottish Programme Director BBC

CONTENTS

TO
WALTER

PROLOGUE

WILLIE

When war broke out in 1914, Willie McFlannel had just completed his apprenticeship as a fitter in a Clyde shipyard. Declining exemption to which his job entitled him, he joined up with the 9th H.L.I. (Glasgow Highlanders), and in due course swaggered home to show off his kilt to his mother, his sister Jeanie, and his two brothers Matthew and George, called Mattha and Geordie for short. Geordie, who had got a lucrative job making munitions and who was hoping the war would last a long time, asked sneeringly if kilties expected men to get up and give them their seats in crowded tramcars, while Mattha, who suffered from corns, knock-knees, and neglected adenoids, remarked that he never knew before what a bandy leggit shauchly wee nyaff his brother was. He pronounced it ' dyaff,' of course, but the word is equally uncomplimentary no matter how it is pronounced. Jeanie, for her part, was only interested in the vast amount of material used for the garment, and as for his mother (a subdued woman who would not live to see the end of the war), she was vaguely surprised that her son should fling up a good job when everybody knew that the war would be over by Christmas. Their home was a two-roomed flat known in Glasgow as a ' room-and-kitchen,' whose only modern convenience was the swan-necked water-tap that dripped ceaselessly into the black sink at the kitchen window.

SARAH

In August 1914 Sarah McTwill was serving in her grandmother's Home Bakery shop by day and going upstairs at night with the old woman to her house above the shop. She was nineteen years old, an unassuming, undistinguished girl who had been glad to leave home two years earlier to escape the constant bickerings of her five sisters. She paid infrequent duty visits to the house of her parents, who bickered with one another as vociferously as their daughters, but Sarah's quiet disposition was at home only with her grandmother. Old Mrs. McTwill was a shrewd native of Aberdeen, unreconciled to Glasgow in spite of having lived in it since her marriage fifty years before. She was a widow now, carrying on her husband's business with the help of a manager, yet doing it with so much secret generosity to impoverished customers that there was never any money for extras in the little house above the shop. Sarah, however, had no fault to find with her lot, for she was in love with a soldier lad who had keeked in at her one day while she was piling cookies in the window, and he was in love with her.

WILLIE AND SARAH

Such, then, was the background of Willie McFlannel and Sarah McTwill who were married on the last day of 1914. To begin with, because Willie was going back to France, they didn't set up house, Sarah remaining with her grandmother in whose house Polly was born in 1916. By the time Matt arrived in 1919, Willie had been demobilized—surprisingly not much the worse physically, and with a D.C.M. ribbon which was not to see the light of day again till the formation of the Home Guard. They found a small flat—a room and kitchen so commodious that it boasted two bed recesses in the kitchen—and there Maisie was born in 1921 and Peter in 1925. By the time Peter was about two years old, quarters had become so cramped that even Willie was forced to admit that a bigger house was advisable, and when a likely one turned up he signed the lease with alacrity.

Ring up the curtain, then, on the home life of a Glasgow working-class family, 1928.

CHAPTER I

WILLIE THE HANDYMAN

WILLIE McFLANNEL, a roll of rather tired-looking linoleum on his shoulder, moved along the gully of tenement houses that was known as Partick Road. Every close was so exactly like its neighbour that he had to peer at each number-plate till he came to the one marked 122; there he turned in, climbed the stairs to the top flat, where he dumped the linoleum on the landing and put a key in the left-hand door. The door open, he dragged the linoleum into the empty house, letting it fall to the floor with a bump that gave him great satisfaction. It was going to be an unpleasant job this, trying to fit old linoleum to a floor with so many knots in the wood; besides, the grate was on the opposite side from their last one, and the bunker was shorter. Ach well! The job had to be done somehow. He took off his jacket.

Two hours later there was a knock at the door. Willie, grumbling, uncoiled himself from his position on the floor and went to open the door. His twelve-year-old daughter Polly brushed past him and came into the house, saying :

' My mammy sent me along to tell you to hurry up ! '

Her father shut the door with an eloquent bang. ' Well, Ah like that ! ' he said. ' An' me workin' like a nigger. Here, see if ye can make yersel' useful. Try an' find a bit waxcloth shaped like a triangle wi' holes cut in it. Ah spent near an hour cuttin' it oot, an' Ah'm blowed if Ah can find it.'

Polly glanced round the kitchen floor perfunctorily. ' Is that it ? ' she asked, giving a kick to the bit nearest her foot.

' Naw ! Ah said wi' holes cut in it ! It's for that bit ablow the jawbox, an' the holes are for the pipes. Jings ! Don't say Ah've to dae the hale thing a' ower again ! '

Together they scrabbled around on the floor for a bit, till Polly said she didn't think it was there.

'But it must be there!' insisted her father. 'Unless Ah've nailed anither bit doon on top o't. Ach, tae hang! Ah wish Ah had the man that invented waxcloth—or linoleum, as yer mother wants us to ca' it. Ah've lost ma temper mair often these last three nights than Ah've ever done afore. Ah thocht the room floor was bad, but this is a fair scunner. What between tryin' to match the pattern, an' cuttin' oot corners that turned oot the wrang wey, an'——'

'Here it is!' exclaimed Polly at last.

'Thank goodness! Noo lay it on the bunker an' staun' ower it fur fear it blows oot the window. Noo, whaur did Ah put that bit chalk? My, it's sickenin' the wey things torment ye by jookin' oot yer sicht! See if ye can find it, Polly. Ah've jist this wee corner in here to finish, an' then that bit ablow the jawbox. An' if you ever see ony sign o' me sayin' Ah'll lay ilecloth again, ye can send fur Geordie Geddes.'

'Who's Geordie Geddes?'

'He's the man that fishes fur corpses in the Clyde. Och, here's the chalk in ma pooch—but whaur's the breidknife noo? It wis there a minute ago. Have you got it?'

Polly was indignant. 'I have not! You told me I wasn't to touch it!'

'So Ah did! That breidknife is guaranteed to cut everything bar waxcloth. Ach, here it's—doon at the bottom o' this pile o' scrap!' Willie squatted on his heels and sharpened the breadknife with a piece of pumice stone. 'It's a wonder yer mother's no' here yet,' he went on. 'No' that Ah'm jist dyin' fur to see 'er, for she'll have as many faults to find wi' ma style o' layin' waxcloth as Ah would hae masel' if Ah wis hur.'

Examining her father's handiwork critically, Polly said: 'She'll not be pleased with you for putting that bit with the hole in it right at the door.'

It was Willie's turn to be indignant. 'Ah couldnae help that!' he snapped. 'You're gettin' as carnaptious as yer mother!'

'You should have put that bit in front of the fire and then it would have been covered with the rug.'

4

The suggestion was so reasonable that it annoyed Willie. 'Look you here!' he said deliberately, 'that bit was absolutely *askin'* fur to be laid there. It fitted perfectly, except fur bein' an inch short—an' that's in the shadow.'

'It won't be in the shadow when the gas is lit.'

'Ach, stop greetin'. A man runnin' fur 'is life'd never see it.'

'Did you ever see a man running for his life, Dad?'

'Don't you be cheeky!' yelled Willie, 'or Ah'll take ma haun' offa your jaw. If that's the kinna thing they learn ye in the Higher Grade, it's time yer were oot workin'. When Ah wis your age Ah wis runnin' messages an' risin' at three in the mornin' fur to pit oot stair lights.'

For a few minutes Willie worked silently with the breadknife and the linoleum, while Polly climbed up on the sink and gazed down at her contemporaries on the tops of the washing-houses far below. Suddenly there was a splutter from the floor.

'Ach, tae hang! Look whit ye've went an' made me dae! Ah've cut this corner oot that wrang wey again. You an' yer Higher Grade! Here, see's anither bit waxcloth.'

At that moment the doorbell rang; Polly leapt from the sink and scuttled through the litter on the floor to open the door for her mother, while Willie mentally prepared himself for a lecture. By the time his wife entered the kitchen he was a model of concentration, hammering away as though his safety depended on his exertions. Mrs. McFlannel was out of breath.

'Oh dear,' she panted. 'I thought I was never going to get here! What a time I've had of it! Is there not a place where I can sit down to get my breath back?'

Without looking up Willie pointed to the sink. 'Sit up on the jawbox there,' he suggested.

'Don't be silly!'

'Would ye like me to help ye up?'

'No. Get on with your work. Are you not near done yet?'

'Och, Ah'm no' that faur aff it,' said Willie amicably; then, to avoid further cross-examination, he asked, 'Whit kept ye? Ah wis expectin' ye an hour ago.'

But his wife was not so easily side-tracked. 'My goodness,

Willie,' she exclaimed, ' what a mess you've made—hardly ever matched the pattern ! '

' Well, Ah done ma best—— '

' And would you look at that big hole—right at the very door ! After me telling you—— '

' Ye can cover it wi' a rug,' interrupted Willie, eager to oblige, ' or wait ye ! Ah'll put in a neat wee patch that'll never be seen. What've ye been doin' wi' yersel' a' this time ? '

' Just like a man ! ' exclaimed Sarah, ignoring the red herring on the conversational track. ' Just like a man ! A patch'll never be seen ! What have *you* been doing with *your*self all this time ? I could've had the job done long ago ! '

With a spurt of anger Willie snapped, ' Do you realize that afore Ah could start layin' waxcloth in the hoose at all, Ah had to hammer doon an' pu' up hunners o' tacks ? An' forbye, a man disnae feel jist as fresh as paint when 'is day's work's done, an' then has tae tackle a flittin'.'

But his wife, womanlike, was unimpressed by masculine worries. ' Oh, I'll need to get a seat,' she wailed. ' I'm just like to drop ! ' Going over to the coal-bunker she lifted the lid, folded down the front leaf, and sat on the edge. Willie, fearful for his precious piece of triangular linoleum, set up a yell that brought Sarah to her feet as quickly as though she had been stung. When calm was restored he asked once again, ' What kept ye ? '

This time she fell into the trap. ' What didn't keep me ! ' she moaned. ' First of all Matt blooded his nose in a fight and I couldn't get the bleeding stopped. And then my sister Maggie ran up to tell me her man's working late to-morrow night and we'll not have him to help us with the flitting.'

' Don't let that worry ye,' murmured Willie. ' Ah've seen him at flittin's afore this.'

' And then my sister Polly that was to be up sure at half-past six to keep the children and let me along here—she didn't turn up till half-past seven—quite joco she was too ! '

Willie was only half-conscious of all the domestic details that flowed down upon him from the bunker-seat, but he managed

6

to remark that he hoped she had given her sister a piece of her mind.

'I couldn't very well do that when she was obliging me !' was the retort.

'Huh ! It's well seen it wisnae *ma* sister !'

'None of your impiddence ! And you can be getting on with your work while I'm speaking.' The fact that she herself was idle didn't seem to worry her. She went on : 'And to crown all, I went up just now to see the coalman about being along with his lorry at six o'clock sharp to-morrow night, and, if you please, he's taken on another flitting before ours, and he'll not be up at us till eight. "Eight o'clock !" says I. "What do you take us for ? It's not a moonlight we're doing !"'

Willie sniggered, aware at the same time of the fact that his wife, with her complete lack of any sense of humour, was unconscious of having said anything to amuse him. 'Whit did the coalman say to that ?' he asked.

'He just said he was sorry. He knows fine that every other coalman's booked up, seeing it's the May term, and that we're in his hands. It's fair aggravating, so it is !'

'Ach, cheer up. Ye never died a winter yet !'

Her husband's philosophy riled Sarah. 'I wish to goodness you'd stop saying that ! It's daft !'

For a moment or two nothing was heard but the tap-tap of Willie's hammer, then Sarah broke out again : 'And that's not the best of it. Imagine—I broke three of my wedding china cups this afternoon. Three of them ! And they were the only ones I had that weren't cracked ! I just sat down and cried like to break my heart. I've got twelve plates and eleven saucers, and now I've only got five cups and they're all cracked !'

Willie didn't appear to be greatly moved by his wife's woes, but all the same he said, 'Poor auld Serah ! We'll jist need to get mairrit a' ower again, an' ye can get another weddin' china set.'

Sarah was disgusted, and said so in one syllable ; Willie, undaunted, went on : 'Would ye mairry me again if ye had the chance ?'

7

'Don't be silly! I've no time for your nonsense and it the flitting to-morrow.' She broke off. Something had caught her eye. 'Here! Did you ever! You don't mean to tell me you've nailed down the linoleum and forgotten to put the paper down first!'

'Whit paper?'

'That pile of newspapers you're kneeling on! Of all the glaiket——'

Willie cut short her epithets. 'Ye never said newspapers to me!' he grumbled. 'And Ah thocht ye'd left this bundle for a cushion for ma knees.'

Shifting her position on the edge of the bunker-front, Sarah said, with determination, 'Well, you'll just have to lift all the linoleum again and put down that paper.'

'Ah'm blowed if Ah will! Whit good is stale news tae a lot o' wee bugs that cannae read?'

'Just you do what you're told and be quick about it!' ordered Sarah, 'for I want to scrub this floor to-night!' Her new position brought into view the antics of Polly perched on the sink. 'Polly!' she exclaimed. 'Come down and get me a pail.'

Polly merely shuffled nearer the window to get a better view of the fun and games in the back court below, while Willie sat back on his heels.

'See here, Serah,' he said, with a grand air of patience, 'who's boss in this hoose? You or me?'

'But——'

'There's nae buts aboot it. Ye're awful fond o' sayin' ye're glad ye havenae got the kinda man that'll staun' bein' henpecked. Well, here's yer chance tae prove it. Whit earthly difference could a sheet o' newspaper make?'

'It's to keep the marks of the floorboards from coming through,' retorted Sarah with an equal display of tolerance, adding, 'and it's supposed to be good for moths.'

'Serah McFlannel, you're too good a housewife to let ony moths get at the waxcloth.'

'You're not going to get round me by flattering!' she retorted adamantly.

'Ach, Serah, ye're wearin' yersel' tae daith worryin' aboot things that don't maitter a docken ! ' He cleared his throat and went on gallantly : ' Ye'll lose a' yer guid looks if ye cairry on like that ! '

The left-handed compliment was too much for her. ' Ugh, you're an awful man,' she said, and turned her back on him. ' Polly ! Stop making faces at the window there and bring me that pail from the lobby press. I can start scrubbing the bits that are nailed down.' As she spoke, she fumbled in her message bag. ' Here ! ' she exclaimed, ' don't tell me I've come away without the scrubbing-brush. Isn't that terrible ! Polly, hen, run you away home as fast as you can and get me that brush. I must've left it on the dresser. Now run ! '

Polly came away reluctantly from her ring-side seat. ' All right,' she muttered. ' And after that can I get out to play ? '

' You can not ! The very idea ! Talking about play and it the flitting to-morrow ! Away you go and hurry up ! '

But before the girl got the length of the door, the bell rang ; opening the door she found a gaunt hag of a woman standing there. ' Is yer mother in ? ' queried the newcomer.

Polly ran back to the kitchen. ' Mammy,' she called, ' there's somebody at the door wanting to see you ! ' Without waiting for an invitation, however, the woman followed Polly and now stood in the kitchen.

' Ah'm Mrs. McTweed ! ' she announced. ' Me an' ma man lives doon ablow. Ah've came up fur to see if there's nae sign o' this bang-bang-bangin' stoppin'.'

From the tone Sarah surmised that Polly would be better to be out of earshot, so she reminded the girl of the urgent need of the scrubbing-brush ; when the door was shut she turned to the woman and said, ' Oh, there's not that much to do now. I'm sorry if you've been annoyed.'

' Annoyed ! Ah should think Ah have. Ma man's a baker an' goes oot at four in the mornin', an' he hasnae had a wink o' sleep this last week fur youse folks ham-ham-hammerin'.'

Sarah was on the point of reminding the lady that they had only had the house for three days, but Willie got in first with,

' Ah'm sorry for that, missus, but we had to get the waxcloth doon.'

' Oh, it's jist waxcloth, is it ? '

The contemptuous look riled Sarah. ' It's nothing of the kind waxcloth ! ' she put in. ' It's the best inlaid linoleum ! '

' It's gey sair worn,' observed Mrs. McTweed. ' Don't tell me ye've a fam'ly.'

' We have that ! Four ! '

' Four ! Whitna disgrace ! Did ye tell the factor ye had a' that size o' a fam'ly ? '

' Of course we did ! We're not ashamed of it. And although I say it myself as shouldn't, they're the best-behaved children in the land. That was Polly, the eldest, you saw just now. She's at the Higher Grade and she's learning the piano.'

Mrs. McTweed folded her arms. ' Pianna ! ' she ejaculated. ' Whit next ! Ah hope it's no' yin o' thae tin-can rattly kinna piannas ! '

' It is not ! My Auntie Jeanie left it to me in her will, and it was tuned just two years ago, wasn't it, Willie ? '

Willie shuffled some bits of linoleum uncomfortably, but he knew what was expected of him as a husband, so he dutifully replied, ' Ay. Oh ay.'

' But,' interrupted Mrs. McTweed, ' Ah cannae get away wi' the factor lettin' youse have the hoose an' youse wi' sichna size o' a fam'ly ! This has always been sichna quiet close. Ah'm tellin' you—there'll be ructions if Ah catch yer weans chalkin' the walls.'

' They'll not do that ! ' insisted Sarah. ' They've always been used to wally walls in a close.'

Visibly impressed, Mrs. McTweed wanted to know where they were coming from, to which Sarah retorted : ' What do you want to know for ? '

' Oh, nothin'. Jist you speakin' aboot wally closes made me wonder if youse were flittin' from Shawlands or Kelvinside or some o' thae high-class districts.' Turning to Willie she asked point-blank, ' Whit dae you dae, mister ? '

Sotto voce, Sarah muttered that he minded his own business, but Willie was feeling affable. 'Ah'm a fitter, missus—at least Ah thocht Ah wis till Ah started layin' waxcl—— ehm, linoleum.'

'He's a leading hand!' interjected Sarah, 'and it'll not be long till he gets his foreman's hat. Is there anything else you'd like to know before I get on with the washing of this floor?'

'Ay!' Mrs. McTweed, unaffected by Sarah's antagonism, leaned against the bunker. 'Ah want to know whether you'll take Friday or Saturday for yer day in the washin'-hoose?'

Sarah was dumbfounded. 'Friday or Saturday!' she repeated. 'I never washed on a Friday or a Saturday in my life, and I'm not going to start now. Monday's my day for washing.'

'Ye cannae get the washin'-hoose on a Monday—that's ma day, an' Ah'm the auldest neebur.'

'Well, what about Tuesday?'

'Ah like that!' Mrs. McTweed's indignation knew no bounds. 'No' right flitted in an' ye're wantin' the best days o' the week for the washin'-hoose. Naw. Tuesdays *and* Wednesdays *and* Thursdays is a' bookit. Forenoon *and* efternoon. So it's Friday or Saturday for you.'

'B-but I never washed all my married life on any other day but a Monday!'

'Ye can go on washin' on a Monday if ye like, but no' in the washin'-hoose, an' ye can dry yer claes on yer kitchen pulleys.'

'Kitchen pulleys!' spluttered Sarah. 'Let me tell you, my washing's not the kind I need to hide on my kitchen pulleys—it can stand peering at as well as other folks'! I'll see the factor about this.'

The threat made no impression on Mrs. McTweed. 'Jist as ye like,' she said calmly; 'but Ah'm the auldest neebur an' Ah've got the maist say. An' anither thing—Ah hope ye'll see an' wash the stairs right doon tae the close-mooth efter yer flittin's in.'

'Thank you! I don't need anybody to come here and tell me what to do. I've never yet had one single complaint from any of my neighbours—but they knew their manners.'

Mrs. McTweed was stung at last. 'Are you suggesting——'
she began, when Sarah cut her short.

'The only thing I'm suggesting is that I'd like to wash that
bit of floor you're standing on.'

'Ah don't think *your* manners are up to much !'

'Here,' said Sarah, 'come and I'll show you where we keep
the outside door,' and, propelled by a strong arm, Mrs. McTweed
was forced to retire. The banging of the door echoed throughout the whole stairway.

Sarah stormed back into the kitchen. 'Did you ever hear
the like of that !' she blazed. 'The bizzum ! Standing there
ordering me about ! And you sitting there on your hunkers,
never letting dab !'

It was Willie's chance now. He seized it. 'Ah nearly let
dab when you came oot wi' that bit aboot me an' the foreman's
hat. Ah wish tae goodness, Serah, ye'd shut up aboot that. If
ony o' the men in the work heard ye they'd hae a fine laugh at
me behind ma back.'

'But it's true !' protested Sarah. 'You're next for the
foreman's job !'

'Och ay, but don't talk aboot it.' For a while nothing was
said between them till Willie dragged himself along the floor to
the sink. 'Well,' he peched, 'here goes for this bobby-dazzler
o' a bit ablow the jawbox here. Ah'll have tae lie on ma
bel—— on ma stummuck tae dae it.'

After that the air was filled with his groans as he struggled to
hammer in tacks within so restricted an area.

'Friday or Saturday !' ruminated Sarah. 'I like that !'

One arm cuddling the waste-pipe, Willie squeezed himself
round to say, 'Whit fur did ye go an' say we lived up a wally
close ? An' you aye girnin' aboot whitna dirty close it is !'

'Ugh. That was just for effect.'

'Ay—the same kinna effect as us gettin' wur second-hand
pianna f'ae your Auntie Jeanie in 'er will !' But the taunt
went unheeded. Suddenly Willie gasped, 'Here ! Whaur's a'
this water comin' f'ae ?'

'What water ? Och—sakes alive !' exclaimed Sarah as she

saw a pool of water at her feet. She kilted her skirts. 'Don't say we've got a burst pipe !'

'Jings, we'll be flooded oot in five meenits at this rate. Ma troosers is soakit a'readies. Whit can it be ?'

Together they peered into the darkness beneath the sink ; then Sarah asked suspiciously, 'Are you sure you haven't knocked a hole in one of these pipes ?'

Willie had had that nasty impression himself, but he made a formal protest. 'Fur ony favour don't say that ! Here, see's a match !' He rolled over on his side, fumbled in his pocket for his matchbox, and struck one match after another without producing a light. 'They musta got wet in ma pooch !' he complained. 'It'll be this pipe here. Feel it.'

Kneeling in the growing puddle of water, Sarah felt it. 'Oh my, my !' she wailed. 'And the flitting to-morrow !'

'Can ye see whaur it's comin' f'ae ?'

'Uhha. It's a hole just where the pipe comes through the floor. Oh my, my ! What'll we do ?'

'Here's ma red hanky. Can we no' tie it——'

Sarah elbowed the offensive piece of red cotton away from her. 'Hanky your granny ! That'll do no good. You put your thumb on the hole till I get a plumber. Oh my, isn't this just awful ! D'you think I should get a policeman ?'

'Naw !' said Willie, rolling over on his stomach once again and reaching out towards the miniature geyser with his thumb. 'The wife doon the stair'll dae that when she sees 'er ceilin'.'

At the memory of Mrs. McTweed, Sarah gasped, 'Oh, her !' She felt paralysed with dread.

'Away doon tae the close-mooth an' see if there's a notice up sayin' whaur the plumber steys,' ordered Willie. 'An' hurry ! Ma thoomb's no' made o' cahootchy.' He screwed his head round to yell after her retreating figure, 'Leave the door aff the sneck ! Ah'll no' be able tae leave this geezer tae open it fur ye.' His voice rose to a crescendo, 'Run ! Ah'm soaked tae the skin a'readies.'

Left alone he told himself that he was fed up, that as sure as death the plumber would be at his mother-in-law's funeral and would be too happy to leave the festivities. For some minutes he pondered the enormity of his carelessness in not watching out for the water-pipes ; he was genuinely sorry for his wife, trachled as she was with the impending flitting ; then, bit by bit his limbs grew stiff till he was one large ache. Jings ! his foot was going to sleep. What could he do ? He daren't get up to stamp it. His pechs broke out afresh as he tried, with his free hand, to smack the leg that was now ' all pins and needles.' He tried shifting his position, only to knock his head against the floor of the sink. The culmination of exasperation occurred when the doorbell rang. Blast it ! It could only be that woman from below !

'Come in, come in !' he yelled, banging his head once again with the force of his oratory.

Mrs. McTweed was in the kitchen so quickly that she could hardly have waited for his invitation. 'Have youse got a burst pipe here ?' she bawled.

'Naw,' cried Willie. 'That's the wey we aye wash wur floors.'

'Nane o' yer impiddence ! D'you know the water's comin' pourin' doon ma shutters like a burn, an' the ceilin's dreepin' wi' water tae the bedplace near.'

Willie tried to soothe her. 'Ah'm daein' ma best, missus.' But she refused to be soothed.

'Ah've got ma floor covered wi' basins an' pails. An' ma man had tae get up oota 'is bed, an' him a baker, an' you lyin' there never botherin' yersel' !'

'Never botherin' masel' ! Ah'm tellin' ye, missus, if Ah took ma thoomb affa this hole ye'd get the hale o' Loch Katrine doon on ye.'

The woman retreated to a drier portion of the floor. 'Have ye sent fur the plumber ?' she demanded.

'The wife's away as fast as she can. Ah'm sorry aboot yer ceilin'.'

'Ye're no' as sorry as me. It wis white-washed jist last month. It's a black-burnin' shame, so it is. Ah've a guid mind tae get the polis tae ye. It's been nothin' but a fair pandemonium since ever ye took this hoose.' She retreated farther until she had reached the lobby. ' Ah'll need tae away an' tell the rest o' the neighbours tae gather water if the plumber's gonnae screw it aff.'

As she disappeared Willie called out, ' Heh ! Don't shut the door ! ' But she did—thoroughly. Willie let his head flop on to the crook of his arm. Ach—she was a dumpling. How would Sarah and the plumber get in now ? Was there any point in lying there in that puddle ? For a few minutes he stayed where he was, too miserable to move, but at last he rose just as the doorbell rang. Soaked to the skin, splashing through water and dripping at every step, he went to open the door. Sarah bounced in.

' Ye werenae long,' he said. ' Whaur's the plumber ? '

' He's screwing the water off at the close,' she panted. ' Oh, what a mess ! I should've told you to gather water for to-morrow.'

Willie contemplated the pond on the floor. ' Is whit's there no' enough ? ' he asked.

' Ah-you ! See—give me a hand to mop this up. Oh dear-dear ! I wish I'd never said I would flit. My feet are soaking.'

' So's ma next week's washin',' observed Willie.

Sarah paused in her wringing to examine her husband. ' Oh, poor soul ! ' she murmured. ' You're like a drowned rat ! What am I to do with you ? '

' Whit aboot hangin' me up on the pulley ? Here—Ah had a visit f'ae the wife doon the stair. It's a peety aboot her man havin' tae get oota 'is bed an' him a baker. She says 'er ceilin's wasted.'

' What a lie ! There's nothing wrong with her ceiling. Her door was standing open when I came up the now, so I keeked into her kitchen.' Just then the doorbell rang. Sarah tut-tutted with irritation as she wrung another clothful of water into the sink. ' Who'll that be next ? I hope it's not that bizzum again ! '

Willie opened the door and Polly rushed in, too excited to

notice anything unusual about her father's appearance. 'Oh, Mammy, Mammy!' she gulped. 'Come on home quick! My Auntie Polly was burning thon old photos and the chimney's on fire. The bobby's away for the butts.'

For a moment or two the three of them gaped speechlessly at one another till Sarah found her voice.

'Oh dear-dear!' she sobbed. 'What are we to do first?'

'Ye cannae expect me tae go through the streets like this!' said Willie.

For the first time since she had come into the house Polly really looked at her father, and the sight made her giggle. 'Oh, Daddy!' she said. 'You're in a rare state for putting out a fire!'

'Don't you be cheeky!' ordered her mother. Sarah was her own brisk self again. 'See—you come home with me.' She turned to Willie, saying, 'You'd better stay here till it's dark. You can keep yourself warm by wiping up this mess. Thank goodness your jacket's dry. Come on, Polly!'

Down the stairs they ran, along half a dozen streets, and the nearer they got to their old home the greater the number of children they passed, all running in the same direction and yelling, 'A lum on fy-er! A lum on fy-er!' Just as their own close came in sight, the fire brigade birled round the corner and swept on ahead of them. The crowd round the close was thick.

'Wait a minute!' said Sarah, laying a restraining hand on Polly's arm and peering upwards through the sooty smoke that filled the street. 'I don't see any flames coming out the chimney. The fire must've died down.'

'It was making an awful roary noise when I left anyway,' commented Polly as though to justify her actions.

Sarah backed into a shop doorway. 'We'll wait here till the butts go away,' she said, but just at that moment another vehicle, all glittering and glaring and clanging, with brass and red paint and whistles, trundled into the street; more and more children followed it. 'Maybe we'd better go up to the house after all,' said Sarah, 'but I hate the idea of going through that crowd.'

'Well, come on through the back courts,' said Polly. 'I know a place where you can squeeze through the railings.' The girl led the way, but she omitted to tell her mother that the route lay through a 'dunny' stinking with dead cats, over a wall, and down the side of an ashpit before the gap in the railings was reached. The result was that when the time came for Sarah to squeeze her well-upholstered body between two bent iron spikes, she was utterly exhausted. She stuck half-way.

'Oh, Polly!' she moaned. 'I can't move.'

Polly gave her mother a push that helped slightly, but it was quite a few minutes before Sarah was clear of the obstruction. She dusted herself, murmuring, 'I hope nobody saw me.'

With a shrewdness that escaped her mother, Polly opined that everybody would be too busy watching the butts in the front street to be interested in the back court. At last they were stealing along under the ground-flat windows of their own close.

'Shsh!' hissed Sarah unnecessarily, 'these footsteps— are they tramping up or down?'

'Down. Listen. That's the butts away! Come on up.'

'No, wait a minute! I can hear some of the neighbours on the landing still.'

So, until all the doors were shut and the sound of the crowd had died away, Sarah crouched there with her daughter. This was a terrible disgrace—and her so proud of being able to flit from a room-and-kitchen with a Place on the Stair to a two-room-and-kitchen with a bathroom! It took all the shine off things. What had her sister Polly been thinking about to let the chimney catch fire? Right enough, it must have been dirty, but Aunt Polly had always been a thowless creature, and she, Sarah, had been a fool to trust her with anything. Oh well, maybe they should creep upstairs now.

Once inside their own house, Sarah pounced on her sister. 'What kind of carry-on was this?' she demanded.

'It wasn't my fault!' snapped Aunt Polly. 'I was just havin' a wee look at some of the old photos, an' Matt flung a paper on the fire an' it went up the lum. He's needin' a right good leatherin', so he is!'

17

Matt, aged ten, was his mother's favourite, but she was feeling too humiliated to be affectionate. 'Are you never in your bed yet?' she stormed.

Matt wrinkled up his begrutten face and blurted out that he couldn't get to bed because it was full of the flitting, Aunt Polly having taken down the pictures, cleaned them, and piled them on the room bed. By the time this affair had been straightened out, Sarah found that her sister had slipped off home and goodness only knew if she would turn up the next day, she was such a huffy creature.

At that point Maisie, asleep in a clothes-basket, wakened up and yelled for attention; when she had been quietened, wee Peter, hitherto unmissed, arrived home in the care of a policeman. He had run out at the height of the excitement over the fiery chimney—which was something more to settle with Aunt Polly. By the time darkness had fallen, however, and Willie had also returned home surreptitiously, peace settled on the household; all the children were sleeping, and although the floor was bare and the grate decrepit-looking because of Willie's wet trousers hanging on the mantelpiece rod, husband and wife sat down for a midnight chat.

CHAPTER 2

THE NEW FLAT

I⊤ was the calm before the storm, for next morning Sarah was so thrang that even her children steered clear of her. There was watery mince and potatoes for dinner and nothing at all for tea but pieces-and-jelly. At six o'clock several aunts and uncles began to arrive to help in the shifting of the furniture. First of all the mirror-back was removed from the sideboard, and Uncle Mattha volunteered to carry it down to the close, where it proved a source of great delight to the children of the district and had eventually to be carried upstairs again. Drawer by drawer a small chest was carried down and re-erected at such an awkward angle that the neighbours had to protest that they couldn't get out. Wee Maisie and Peter having been toddled along to their granny's to be out of the way, the other two children did their best to make up for the younger ones' absence. The house seemed full of people, of dust, of furniture, of noise. The stairway was cluttered with strange children helping and clamouring to help.

When the confusion was at its height Willie sought his wife. ' Here, is there nae sign o' that coalman ? ' he complained, conveying the impression that the delay was Sarah's fault.

At that Matt, perched on the sink, began to dance and shout, ' Here 'e is, Daddy. Here's the coalman ! Here's the coalman ! Here's——'

When the child had been quietened by the simple expedient of giving him something to carry to the lorry, Sarah exclaimed, ' Willie ! Just you give that coalman a piece of your mind. Fancy—half-past eight instead of six o'clock ! '

But Willie was too relieved by the fact of the lorry's arriving at all to be lured into a quarrel with such an important factor in the proceedings. He addressed the whole company. ' Well, chaps an' fellow-cairters, whit are we puttin' on the lorry first ? '

He glanced around him. 'Here—the feather bed. The very thing the doctor ordered. Come on !'

Sarah watched her husband. 'Do you want me to lift it ?' she asked.

'Naw !' said Willie indignantly, threading his way through a chaos of tin trunks and hampers and orange-boxes. He kicked one of these last, or perhaps it was the box that kicked him. 'Here !' he bawled. 'Whaur did a' this troke come f'ae ?'

'From below the bed,' answered Sarah calmly.

'Ugh away ! Whit's in them ?'

'Never you mind. I'm waiting to see you lifting that feather bed.' She winked at the other ladies of the company and they winked back, all of them folding their arms in eloquent anticipation.

One of the tin trunks reached out and tapped Willie on the shin ; he tapped back with his toe. 'Heh !' he yelled. 'Can ye no' clear some o' this stuff oot the road ?'

One of the men obliged by heaving a hamper on to his shoulder and carting it away, but before Willie could approach the bed his brother Mattha appeared on the scene.

'Heh, Wullie,' he moaned. 'C'm'ere ! Yer kist o' drawers has got jammed in the ootside door. It'll neither come in nor go oot !'

'Whitna scunner ! D'ye think we'll need tae take the door aff ?'

'Ay !' replied Uncle Mattha with mournful satisfaction, 'but hoo are ye gonnae get intae the hinges ? Tell me that ! Ye shoulda ta'en the door aff afore we startit !'

Willie turned his back on the feather bed. 'Jings !' he exclaimed when he saw the mountain of mahogany blocking the doorway. 'Come on an' we'll gie it anither shove. It'll no' maitter if it gets scraped a wee.'

'But it will matter !' protested Sarah. 'That chest belanged to ma mother !' In her excitement she forgot to speak as carefully as befitted one who was about to remove to a two-room-and-kitchen house with a bathroom, and for the rest of the evening her speech remained at the comfortable level of a room-and-kitchen with a Place on the Stair.

'Tae hang wi' yer mother!' retorted Willie. 'Come on an' shove wi' the rest o' us!'

Quite a lot of people shoved, Sarah screamed, the jambs of the door were snapped, two handles (inlaid with mother-of-pearl) flew off; it wasn't until everybody was exhausted that it was discovered the coalman and his three assistants had been under a misapprehension and had been shoving too—from the opposite side. When mutual understanding was established, the chest of drawers was successfully launched on to the stairs, with Sarah's tears for champagne.

'Lea'e it on the landin' there till Ah bring doon the feather bed. It's goin' on the lorry first, mind!' were Willie's instructions; then, catching sight of his wife's tears, he added, 'Ach you! Stop greetin'! Ye cannae expect tae hae a flittin' withoot somethin' gettin' broke!'

He hurried back to the bedside where he wrestled and peched under Sarah's drying eyes, but the more he pulled at the mattress the more it eluded his grasp. At last he called, 'Heh, Mattha, come on you an' see if you can dae onythin' wi' this bag o' tricks!'

Mattha spat on his hands and joined Willie at the bedside. Sarah and her ladies-in-waiting exchanged one-sided smiles. 'Ah'll dae ma best!' promised Uncle Mattha adenoidally. 'But Ah don't want tae rax masel'.'

'Here's the coalman!' exclaimed Willie when he saw how unavailing his brother's efforts were in spite of all his noise. 'Get oot the road, Mattha, an' see whit the coalman can dae wi't.'

The coalman sized up the situation in an instant. 'Staun' oot the road!' he ordered; then, a moment later, 'Heh! Was ony of youse tryin' fur to smother me the now?' But the faces of Willie and Mattha were too concerned to be guilty. He tried again.

Sarah made another offer, but Willie brushed her aside with, 'Get away wi' ye, wumman! If three men cannae dae onythin' wi't—— Whaur's ma brither Geordie? Geordie! Heh!'

Geordie laid down a gasalier which, in order to avoid taking an end of the sideboard, he had been intending to carry down to the lorry; he approached the bed reluctantly. Matt picked up the gasalier. 'Mammy,' he pleaded, 'can I get carrying this down?'

At that moment Polly appeared with a huge framed photograph of Matt in infancy. Before she got the chance to ask her mother's permission to carry it to the lorry, Matt pounced on it yelling his suspicions that she intended showing it to his chums clustered round the close; they would never allow him to forget, he insisted, that he had once lain on a cushion with nothing on him but a cloud of tulle. To settle the ensuing squabble, Sarah sent them off the premises, one with a frying-pan and the other with a discouraged aspidistra.

Just then Willie had an idea. 'Ah tell ye whit,' he exclaimed, kicking the accumulation of boxes which still cluttered his pathway, 'get a' this rubbish oot the road an' then the lot o' us can grab the feather bed at the one time an' pu' it on tae the floor!'

This was too much for Sarah. 'You will not!' she declared. 'See—get outa ma road, the lot of ye! As if a woman didn't know how to handle a feather bed!' With the ease of long experience she flattened out the mass that the men had left, seized it with both arms, and shouted, 'There you are! Get a rope and tie it while I'm holdin' it!'

The men were so aghast with admiration that Aunt Maggie had to fetch the rope. While the mattress was being bound, Matt took the opportunity to ask if he could carry down the rearing black horses from the room mantelpiece, and his anger at her refusal was mingled with the sound of breaking glass, with Willie's inquiries for the whereabouts of the screwdriver that was jutting from his hip-pocket, with Uncle Mattha's complaints that he had a skelf in his finger, and finally with Polly's announcement that she had torn her skirt on a nail.

'Ugh, never mind,' snapped Sarah.

'But look at it, Mammy!' Polly turned round, and so much of her underwear was visible that the skirt had to be tacked together instantly. While Sarah was at the job, Willie sidled up to her.

'That's a fine brother you've got!' he grumbled. 'Look at 'im staunin' there spittin' on 'is hauns an' dodgin' a' the heavy lifts.'

But Sarah wasn't interested; neither did she answer Polly when the girl, trying to establish some kind of human contact in the midst of the mêlée, said, 'Everybody's hanging out of their windows watching the flitting, Mammy.' After all, that was what one expected at a flitting! that was why one spent weeks before the time polishing everything! Sarah stitched away at the little skirt in silence, till Willie returned to report that the coalman had just obliterated the gasalier by stepping back on it on the lorry. Before she could make any comment, Willie went on:

'Whit's worryin' me is that pianna we're supposed tae've got f'ae your Auntie Jeanie in 'er will. Ye widnae like tae gether it in yer arms like the feather bed?'

Sarah broke off the tacking thread, ignoring Willie's pleasantries. She herself had lost quite a lot of sleep over the safety of the instrument. Should she not have taken some precautions to protect the grandeur of the fretwork front? Her hand on her bosom, she watched the men heaving and shuffling and yelling around the piano, out of the room, into the lobby, backwards and forwards, 'Easy there!'—through the lobby into the kitchen doorway, 'Steady, boys!'—out on to the landing, crash into the wall, 'Ah've snecked ma fing-er!'—crash into the staircase window, 'That wis your fault!'—down the stair, down the stair, growling along the close, out on to the lorry, 'Heave!' 'Heave again, lads!' Ah, it was up! Safely.

An hour later the house, for over nine years their home, the birthplace of their children, the despised room-and-kitchen, was empty; Sarah, left alone in it, walked through the echoing rooms. Why was she feeling so queer? Hat and coat on, she went to the window and looked down on the street, at the lorry-load of furniture. Was it possible that that collection of junk could be hers ? Bits of sticks they were—just bits of sticks ! Surely they didn't need to hang the frying-pan at the back like that, inviting as it did the attentions of a small boy with a spoon (where had he got it ?). He was making a terrible din.

That was the lorry away now—Willie, with the coalman, at the horse's head, Uncle Mattha sitting on the side with a pile of basins on his knee (allow him to make himself comfortable !), Uncle George at the rear with the coalman's assistants, chasing off children who wanted to follow. Where were the others ?

Oh well, the worst part of the job was still to come ; she had better be getting along. Should she chap at the next door and say good-bye ? Better not, in case the woman thought she was trying to ape the gentry, especially when she was flitting to a two-room-and-kitchen with a bathroom. . . . A last look-round, this time to see if anything had been left. The shutting of the door put an end to her sentimental mood, and by the time she reached her new home she was prepared to cope with all the problems she knew would be waiting for her.

Uncle Mattha, she found, was aggrieved because he hadn't been told the new house was three stairs up. ' Ah wouldnae of came if Ah had of knew,' he insisted.

' Ach, don't greet,' said Willie. ' Ye'll get a drink as soon as we're done.'

To which his brother retorted that a gey few drinks would be needed before tackling the adjectival piano, that he, personally, didn't want to rax himself, that he had his work to think about.

' Ugh, give him a drink the now, Willie,' urged Sarah. Instantly Mattha's face brightened, but when she added, ' There's lots of Iron Brew,' he disappeared with an ' ach ' of disgust. After that there was the problem of the broken overmantel to deal with, the problem of the woman down the stair who wanted to know if there was much more to come up as her man was a baker and couldn't sleep for the noise, and the problem of finding the bread in order to give Matt a piece. It was the sight of the bread-box that had reminded him of his hunger, but as it

was discovered to be full of slippers and cutlery it took some
time to quieten the child's clamour.

'There's jist the pianna left noo, mister,' announced the
coalman, and Willie, rallying his forces, found that his brother
Mattha was missing. Eventually he ran him to earth in the
lobby press and yanked him out, shouting, ' Sarah, you have the
refreshments ready for us when we come back. It disnae matter
if ye havenae tumblers for everybody. Jeely jaurs'll dae ! '

' If it's Iron Brew, a thimblefu'll dae me ! ' moaned Mattha.

The men clattered down the stair, tired but cheerful, while
Polly joined her brother in demanding a piece. At length the
loaf was discovered in a drawer, the jelly jar in the potato bag,
but the bread-knife, hiding amongst some tools in the baikie,
eluded the searchers till the piano was coming in the door.
Everybody rushed to see its triumphal entry into the parlour.

The outside door was slammed with an utter disregard for
the fact that it was now nearly eleven o'clock, while the whole
company—aunts, uncles, nephews, nieces, friends, coalmen, host
and hostess, son and daughter, a stray dog and Uncle Mattha—
crowded into the kitchen. When the Iron Brew, augmented by
lemonade and ginger ale, had been distributed, Willie called for
the toast, ' Here's tae wursel's ! ' There was an instant blatter of
cordiality.

' Willie,' whispered Sarah at the first lull, ' who's the three
strange men ? '

The explanation that they had joined the party within the last
ten minutes as friends of the coalman was no comfort to her,
neither was the sudden sound of a mouth-organ and the
announcement from Uncle Geordie, ' Come on an' hae a wee
sing-song ! ' Before she could protest, suggestions for the
programme poured from all directions. When three separate
concerts had got under way simultaneously, Sarah pleaded with
her husband to insist on everybody going home. ' Give them a
hint about the neighbours,' she added. ' It's that late ! '

Matt, overhearing the remark, asked hopefully, ' Is it twelve
o'clock yet, Daddy ? '

' No' yet, son.'

'What about hangin' up the kitchen clock?' continued Sarah. 'Maybe if you put the hands to twelve o'clock they'd take the hint.'

'Och, onythin' fur a quiet wife!' Willie battled his way through the solid block of humanity, got the steps from the bathroom, and fought his way back again to the fireside. One or two guests got knocked about a bit, but as the company was then engaged in singing 'The bonnie wells o' Wearie' no notice was taken; the casualties, being Rangers supporters, probably imagined themselves at a football match against the Celtic. Sarah followed with the clock, saying:

'Oh dear-dear! This is terrible! What'll the neighbours think!'

Willie, with difficulty, got the steps spread, and, with still greater difficulty, mounted them and reached down for the clock. 'Ah hope tae goodness it disnae take yin o' thae turryvees an' stop strikin' for a week,' he remarked, as he fumbled for the nail high up on the frieze. 'There's never been a spring cleanin' yet that it hasnae stopped strikin'. Ups-a-daisy! There she goes! Is that straight?'

From her position immediately below, Sarah peered upwards. 'A wee bit to the left,' she advised. Willie made the adjustment, and she added, 'Now put the hands to twelve o'clock!'

'They're p'intin' tae eight o'clock, but!'

'Never mind. As long as the folk here see the time.'

'But that'll mix up the strikin', wumman!'

'It can't be helped. You do what you're told!'

So the hour-hand was shifted up beside the other one at the figure XII. The clock began to strike, but only Matt heard it; sitting on a footstool he chanted, 'It's twelve o'clock! It's twelve o'clock! I've never been up so late before! It's twelve . . .'

Willie, high up on his perch at the top of the steps, counted with the strokes, 'Nine, ten, eleven, twelve . . .'

'That's thirteen!' called Polly.

'Whit the dickens!' gulped Willie as the clock went on

striking, Polly and Matt accompanying it—'sixteen, seventeen, eighteen, nineteen.'

'Here, shut up,' yelled Willie to the choristers who had now struck up a fresh ditty. 'Shut up! You an' yer auld Scots sangs! Listen tae this!'

But nobody heeded him save Polly and Matt—'twenty-one, twenty-two, twenty-three.'

At that point Uncle Mattha came to life; he laid his untasted tinnyful of ginger ale on the bunker. 'Whit's up?' he ejaculated. 'Oh, jings! Is it that time a'readies? Ah'll be late fur ma work!' Dispensing with the formality of shaking hands with his hosts and fellow-guests, he left the house just as Sarah, in despair, was calling, 'Willie, for any sake, *do* somethin'. Stop the clock!'

'Ay, but how? Take aff the pendulum?'

'Twenty-nine, thirty, thirty-one, thirty-two . . .' chanted the children.

'Tae hang wi' you an' yer blasted mooth-organ!' bellowed Willie at last. '*Shut up!*'

The singing dwindled and finally ceased; the clock continued striking. 'Aw help!' exclaimed the coalman, 'the nock'll no' stop strikin'!' He joined Polly and Matt—'thirty-seven, thirty-eight . . .'

Uncle Geordie and Aunt Maggie took up the chorus—'thirty-nine, forty, forty-one . . .'

'Oh my, is this no' terrible!' wailed Sarah. 'What'll the neighbours think! That bizzum doon the stair'll be up any minute.'

By this time the whole company were counting together, echoing each strike with a stamp on the floor—'forty-five, forty-six, forty-seven . . .'

There was a sound of muffled knocking on the wall. 'Willie! D'ye hear that?' called Sarah. 'That's the folk through the wall—up the next close—knockin' on us. Ye'll have to do somethin'! Stop the clock when I tell ye!'

'Ach, we'll let it go tae fifty.'

But it went beyond fifty—quite a bit.

'Oh dear-dear!' Sarah was on the verge of tears. 'I'll

never be able to lift ma head outside after this. The neighbours'll think we're from the slums.'

Once again the knocking sounded on the wall; Willie knocked back to show there was no ill-feeling.

'Sixty-one, sixty-two, sixty-three . . .' counted the company in mounting glee and with heavier footwork, '. . . seventy-five, seventy-six . . .'

Some of the more sophisticated members of the party fell out of the chant to transact a little business on the clock's prospects of attaining a century; altogether sevenpence-halfpenny had changed hands, when the clock suddenly stopped at ninety-eight. Willie, still seated on the top of the steps, felt a personal pride in the achievement. 'Hurray!' he cried lustily. 'Ninety-eight! No' bad for an auld clock!'

'Three cheers for the auld nock!' shouted the coalman. 'Hip! Hip! Hooray!'

As the yells died away there was a thunderous battering at the door. 'Oh dear-dear!' moaned Sarah again. 'What'll we do if that's the polis?'

At the word polis several of the company showed a marked desire to be home, while one or two made a hurried investigation of the hiding capacity of the lobby press.

'I'm frightened to go to the door!' declared Sarah.

'Ah'll go!' said Willie as he reached the floor. 'Ah'm no' feart fur the polis!' and if there was a studied emphasis on the pronoun nobody took up the challenge.

In a few moments, clear as a bell, the voice of Mrs. McTweed tolled throughout the house, the landing, and the stairway: 'Whitna-like hallabaloo is this? Ah never heard the like in a' ma born days! Ma man's a baker an' hasnae had a wink o' sleep since youse folks took the hoose. There's only wan wey tae stop it. Ah'm away fur the polis!'

With the eagerness of relief the company poured out of the house, down the stairs, carrying Mrs. McTweed with them on the breast of the current. Willie was left alone at the door. Shutting it, he went back into the kitchen where he found his wife in the throes of humiliation.

'What did I tell ye!' she sobbed. 'It's all your fault. I don't know what the neighbours'll think! Oh dear-dear! And me wantin' to be that genteel!' She sank down into a basket-chair and wept unrestrainedly; Polly and Matt, frightened by this new picture of their mother, plucked at her skirts and cried too.

Willie was bewildered. Gruffly, to hide his feelings, he said, 'Ach, stop greetin'. There's nae harm done. This is gonnae be a terrible-like place tae bide in if ye cannae hae a wee bit fun at a flittin'. We'd a been better tae've steyed whaur we were if this is the kinna thing we're tae hae fur the rest o' wur lives.'

His complaint was as oil poured upon the fire of Sarah's own doubts; she flared up, her tears forgotten. 'That's right! Blame me for comin' here! A fine father you are—wantin' to bring up your family in a room-and-kitchen wi' a Place on the Stair. You that's always talkin' about——'

Willie cut her short. 'Haud yer wheesht!' he ordered. 'It's time the weans was in bed.'

Taking the hint Sarah soon had supper made, and afterwards Polly was tucked up in an improvized bed in the bedroom, with Matt in a similar contraption in the parlour. It was the first time in their lives that the children had slept by themselves; it would probably be the last for many a night to come since wee Maisie and Peter would be joining them the next night, but they were too sleepy to be thrilled by the experience. Around half-past twelve husband and wife drew up their chairs to the fireside, Willie to have a smoke and Sarah to make a thorough job of mending Polly's skirt. They sat in silence for a while, then Willie said awkwardly, 'Ehm . . . Serah, Ah'm sorry fur . . . fur . . .'

'Shsh, Willie, it was my fault. I shouldn't have spoken to you like that in front of the children. It was just that . . . that . . . I wanted to make a good impression right at the start in front of my new neighbours, and here——'

'Ay, Ah know. But ye'll can put that right the morn. Ye'll soon be twistin' them roon yer wee fing-er the same wey that ye twist me.'

'Ach away ! I'm sure I'm always saying you're the boss in the house.'

'Ay—when you're oot ! '

Knocking the dottle from his pipe, Willie fetched the steps from beneath the clock. He spread them at the glaring window and climbed up to cover its nakedness with sheets of brown paper. Sarah, having finished the mending of the little skirt, unleashed the feather bed.

CHAPTER 3

ENTER LASSIE

SOMETHING wakened Matt. What was it? Stiff with fear, he lay listening. Where was he? What were all those queer shapes sticking around him in the faint light from the street lamps far below? He hid his head quickly beneath the bed-clothes, till he remembered about the flitting. He came up for air. It was terribly quiet. Not even a clock was ticking. But still he was frightened. Why? For a while he stared at the odd shadows on the ceiling.

Suddenly he flung off the blankets. Stumbling and screaming he rushed in the direction of the kitchen, yelling, 'Mammy! Daddy! Mammy, where are you?'

There was an answering shout from his mother that guided him into the strange darkness of the kitchen. Willie, befuddled with sleep, turned over on his other side, mumbling and groaning.

'What's wrong, son?' called Sarah from the back of the enclosed bed.

'Mammy! Mammy! There's somebody in the room.'

'Ach away! You've been dreaming!'

Still Matt trembled and stammered. 'But there is, Mammy! I heard him—laughing and crying.'

'Whit's that?' asked Willie, waking up.

'Matt says there's somebody in the room.'

'Naw!'

The incredulity in his father's voice made Matt forget to be sorry for himself. 'But there is!' he yelled. 'In below the sofa!'

'Ach, ye're dreamin', son. Naebody could get in ablow the sofa. It's too near the grun'.' Willie believed in reasoning with his children, even at three o'clock in the morning.

'Away you back to bed, son,' advised Sarah affectionately. 'You've maybe had a bad dream.'

'But I *was*n't dreaming! I was waken when I heard it!'

31

Sarah poked her husband. ' You go ben and let him see there's nobody there,' she ordered.

' Ach ! . . . Whaur's the matches ? ' Willie disentangled himself from the bed-clothes, pushed his feet into his slippers, and, the matchbox in his hand, groped through the lobby to the parlour. Matt, however, remained by his mother.

' Away you go, Matt,' she said coaxingly, wearily. ' D'you want me to come and tuck you in again ? '

' No. I don't want to go back there.'

Sarah heaved herself out of the bliss of the feather bed. Discipline had to be maintained, especially in a two-room-and-kitchen house. Throwing a bed-mat round her shoulders she led Matt, protesting, towards the parlour. There they found Willie, a lighted match in his hand, going round the room.

' Look, son,' he said. ' There's naeb'dy here. Come on away back tae yer wee beddie-baw.'

' No ! I don't want to hear thon noise again.'

' Whit kinna noise wis it ? '

Matt cleared his throat and gave what nobody recognized was a fairly good imitation of a dog barking in its sleep. Husband and wife looked at each other in the flickering matchlight. ' Ach, ye've been dreamin' ! ' said Willie. ' There's nae sich noise. Sure there isnae, Mammy ? '

Sarah, bone-weary, ached for bed. ' Ach, come on,' said she. ' He can sleep at the foot of our bed to-night. He'll be all right to-morrow night when wee Peter's here and they're both in the bed. It's him being sleeping on the sofa that's upset him. Come on, son. Come on, Willie.'

Because it was Saturday the household was late in rising the next morning. Willie was on ' short time.' The four of them were seated at breakfast when the door creaked. Matt jumped in his chair.

' What's up with you now ? ' demanded his mother.

' The door ! ' murmured Matt, wide-eyed. ' The door's opening ! '

And so it was, slowly, and for no apparent reason. Then gradually, about six inches from the ground, a small black snout appeared, followed timidly by a hairy little face lit by two bright eyes.

'A rat!' gasped Sarah, petrified.

Polly, from her seat at the far side of the table, saw more than the others—a lifted, uncertain forepaw, a shrinking little body, ending in a ragged but plucky tail.

'Oh, a wee puppy!' she shrieked delightedly.

'A puppy?' echoed Matt.

Both of them bounded to the door, but the dog, scared, raced for the shelter of the parlour and had taken refuge below the sofa before they reached it. Willie was on the heels of his children. 'Whaur is it?' he demanded. The three of them peered under the sofa making coaxing noises of all kinds, but the frightened dog merely growled in response. 'That beast's scared tae daith,' said Willie, lying flat on his front. 'Serah!' he yelled. 'Bring us a saucer o' milk.'

'I'll do nothing of the kind!' came back the indignant reply. 'Kick it down the stair.'

'Aw, Serah, ye widnae see the puir beast starvin'! It musta came in wi' the flittin' last night.'

'Well, the sooner it's out the better I'll be pleased. Come on, you, and finish your porridge.'

'Jist a meenit.' Once again Willie tried to persuade the little animal to come out, but it refused all overtures. 'Ah tell ye whit,' whispered Willie to his children. 'Away you two go ben the hoose. Shut this door efter ye. It's maybe feart fur a crood.'

Matt was reluctant to leave. 'Three's not a crowd!' he declared in defiance of the popular belief to the contrary.

'You dae whit ye're tellt!' There was that in their father's voice which made the children get up and leave the room. Willie, still stretched on the floor, gazed back into the two brown eyes in the shadow. His workmates would not have recognized his tones as he murmured, 'Puir wee dog! Are ye lost? Whit are ye frightened fur? Ah'll no' hurt ye. Nice wee dug. Come on an' speak tae me. Look, ma haun's emp'y. Come on, pet. That's the wey. Come away!'

33

The dog was advancing slowly, when Sarah's voice filtered through from the kitchen. 'Willie! Come ben at once and finish your porridge. It'll be black cold!'

Instantly the dog retreated to its corner where it flopped down again with a flick of its tail, which was no doubt intended to convey the information that it had no animosity towards Willie personally. He got to his feet and went into the kitchen. 'That dug's starvin'!' he announced, lifting his plate half full of porridge.

Sarah faced him, her eyes blazing. 'Well, you're not going to give it good porridge!'

'Ah'll gie it purritch if Ah like!'

'But how can you do all the work I've got for you the day if you're not fed?'

At that both Polly and Matt stopped pretending to eat and insisted on sacrificing their portion for the sake of the dog. Willie took no notice of them. 'Whit's come ower ye, Serah? Tae think there's a wee beast in there starvin' tae daith an' ye widnae gie it a bite o' meat!'

'I'm wanting no dogs in this house!'

'Neither am Ah! But Ah'd raither hae a live yin than a deid yin.'

With that he left the kitchen, closing the door; he closed the parlour door also before he approached the sofa, where he sprawled on the floor again. 'Come on, pet. Here's somethin' fur tae eat.' Laying down the plate of porridge he separated the congealing mass with his spoon, glad that he had just poured in a fresh supply of milk before the alarm had been raised. 'Come on! Somethin' fur a hungry wee dug!' The dog's snout was moistening, a pink tongue slipped out and performed the duties of a handkerchief. 'That's a wee pet. Come on.' Willie pushed the plate farther in. Ah, it was stretching itself. Just then the kitchen door banged. The dog lay down again growling. Willie got up, leaving the plate where it was, and, closing the door, strode back to the bosom of his family.

'See here, Serah——' he began, when his wife interrupted him.

'Have you pitched that beast down the stair yet?'

'See here, Serah,' he repeated.

'No, I'll not see! The very idea! Bringing a dog into the house and it the flitting! Frightening the life out of Matt.'

Matt protested that he wasn't frightened now, but neither of his parents heeded him.

'Ah never brung the dug intae the hoose!' insisted Willie. 'An' Ah don't want tae keep it. Ah jist want tae keep the thing f'ae starvin' tae daith. Jist gie it a chance tae take the purritch an' then Ah'll pit it oot.'

This last statement brought a howl from the children, Matt proclaiming that if he had known through the night that it was a lonely wee dog that had been crying he would have taken it into the bed beside him—a show of magnanimity that didn't appeal to his mother in the least. Suddenly there was a thumping noise in the lobby. Willie, going to investigate, found that the dog had eaten the porridge and now wanted some fresh air. He opened the outside door, watched the nimble little mongrel scamper down the stair, then went back to the kitchen feeling slightly resentful that it hadn't shown more gratitude.

'Cheer up, Serah, it's away,' he said.

'Good riddance!' Sarah slapped another plateful of porridge on to the table. 'There! I've scraped the pot for you!' Her tone conveyed her disapproval.

'Will it not come back?' asked Matt.

'If that dog comes back here I'll throw a pail of water at it!' said Sarah grimly.

The children gaped at each other in horror, then at their father for sympathy, but he, having satisfied his conscience, seemed no longer interested in the subject.

'Daddy,' said Polly at length, 'is the wee dog lost?'

'Likely. It hadnae a collar on onywey.'

'What kind of a dog is it?'

'Ah'm no' sure. The wee thing's sides were that near yin anither it looked mair like a razor blade than a dug.'

The children intercepted an accusing look pass between their parents.

35

' Aw, Mammy,' cried Matt, ' why can we not keep it ? '

' Just because I said it ! '

' Wheesht, son ! ' advised Willie.

For a while nothing was said until a thumping sound was heard against the outside door.

' It's back ! ' exclaimed both children delightedly.

' There you are ! ' said Sarah. ' I just knew that would happen ! '

' Will I let it in, Mammy ? ' asked Matt.

It was hard to refuse Matt anything, but Sarah was adamant. ' No ! There's no dogs coming into this house ! Let it go home to its own home.'

' But if it's lost ? '

' Well, let whoever it belongs to come and get it ! '

' But, Mammy——' Matt was continuing, when the doorbell rang.

Sarah went to open the door, and she was so surprised to see Granny and wee Maisie and Peter standing there that she didn't notice the dog slipping in at her feet ; and in the general explanation of how Granny had found herself physically unable to cope with her charges, the dog had ample time to make its way back beneath the sofa.

The smell of dinner being served, however, brought it out again, and it set up a heart-rending whimper behind the kitchen door. Sarah was furious, and accused everybody of conspiring against her to smuggle the dog into the house. Willie, protesting his innocence, opened the door and the dog bounded up on his shins. He picked it up as the children, fearful of their mother's wrath, craned forward to see it. There was a scar beneath its right eye, and its left ear, torn in some battle, hung forward like a doggy wink ; the other pricked upwards and backwards in alternate interest and fear. Willie patted the trembling body. ' Puir wee lassie ! ' he crooned. ' Ye're no' tae be feart. We'll no' touch ye. Is't a wee bite o' meat ye're efter ? '

Its nose twitching, the dog yearned towards the food on the table. Sarah got up from her chair. ' Willie ! ' she said, with ominous quiet. ' I want to speak to you. Outside.'

Carrying the dog, Willie left the kitchen and joined his wife in the dishevelled parlour.

' Are you, or are you not, going to put that dog out ? '

' Ach, Serah——' The dog was licking his face, no doubt because his breath was redolent of steak and onions ; but the man found the gesture irresistible.

' D'you not think four children are enough to feed and keep clean ? ' demanded Sarah.

' Ach ay, but——' Once again his face was licked. ' Listen,' he said, ' let it hae somethin' tae eat an' then Ah'll take it oot fur a walk. It'll maybe find its wey hame.'

' And if it doesn't ? '

' Well, Ah could—ehm—put a notice in the sweetie-shop windy.'

' And if it isn't claimed ? '

' Och, time anuff tae worry aboot that.'

' Well ! ' said Sarah. ' Before you say your piece about who's boss in this house, let me tell you—if that dog makes a mess, out it goes ! I'm warning you ! '

With that she marched back into the kitchen, where she found the children seated quietly at the table—too quietly, and it would have taken a keener observer than their mother to have noticed their breathlessness after scuttling from behind the keyhole. Willie followed, carrying the dog. To prevent any danger of the floor being used in an unladylike manner, he kept the animal on his knee. The children crowded round, only to be yanked back into place by their mother.

' Can I get going out with you when you take it for a walk, Daddy ? ' asked Matt, and Willie was too intent on feeding small bits of his steak to the dog to notice anything unusual in his son's acquaintance with his intended movements.

' What d'you think its name is ? ' asked Polly after Matt had been dealt with by his mother.

' Oh, Ah don't know,' said Willie. ' Maybe it's Flossie.' He looked inquiringly at the dog. ' Flossie ? ' he repeated, but the dog merely licked her whiskers and peered hopefully at the other plates. Willie then began to go through a list of all the likely girls' names ; the others joined in and Sarah was helpless to stop the chorus : ' Nellie ! Sally ! Lassie ! Lady ! Sheila ! ' But there was no answering flicker in the face of the animal who was now struggling to reach the scraps Matt was surreptitiously offering it. Polly had once been in a house where a dog was kept.

' D'you think it could lie down and die for its country ? ' she asked.

' The sooner it lies down and dies the better I'll like it ! ' interposed Sarah, clearing away the plates.

Like a flash the dog sprang out of Willie's hands ; it leapt to the floor and raced after Sarah to the sink. She turned round and found it at her feet, looking up wistfully from her face to the pile of plates in her hand ; she hesitated. The dog instantly sat up on its rear, waving its front paws. Everybody was enchanted with the performance—that is, everybody except Sarah.

' Oh, you're a beggar, are you ? ' she said. ' Well, you needn't think I'm going to give you plates to lick that my bairns'll have to eat out of after. So there ! '

To which Polly, fresh from first-year Science at the school, took it upon herself to point out that if the plates were washed in boiling water no harm would be done. But her mother ignored her. Instead she stared at the dog which had now stopped waving its paws and was cocking its head to one side, its pink tongue chasing the slavers dripping from an eager mouth. The children held their breath, torn between watching the dog pleading its cause and watching their mother to see if there were any signs of relenting in her face. Then the dog, weary of sitting in one position so long, let down its front paws and sat, tail a-sweep, gazing up in an agony of desire. Still Sarah stared, hardening her heart.

' Ask 'er again ! ' whispered Willie hoarsely.

Obediently the dog sat up again. Sarah, in spite of herself, gave in. She piled all the scraps on to one plate which she put on the floor, saying :

' There you are ! But I don't like beggars ! '

The family, father and children, looked at one another wonderingly, hopefully. Without a word Sarah went to the cupboard, took out an old basin which she filled with water, and laid down beside the dog. By-and-by, having eaten and drunk, the dog came up to Sarah. Placing one hesitant paw on the woman's leg it wagged its tail.

' Ugh ! ' said Sarah, reaching down and patting the tiny head. ' You're an awful wee beast. Now—that'll do ! '

The others were still afraid to speak, although they all coaxed with clucking fingers and tongues. The dog, however, passed them by ; she made straight for Willie who picked her up.

' We'll need tae see whit we can dae aboot yer face, lass,' said he. ' An' ye'll need tae get a bath. Ye look as if ye'd been in the canawl.'

Instantly there was a clamour for permission to see the dog being bathed, a clamour that almost undid all the good work the dog herself had done on Sarah's hard heart, but Willie silenced them by saying that it had to go for a walk first and perhaps it would find its way home.

' But, Daddy, surely you don't want it to go home ! ' pleaded Matt. ' It's *such* a nice wee puppy ! '

' I think somebody tried to get rid of it and flung it into the canal,' said Polly, while Peter, now as eager as the rest, pointed out that if any folk had been as cruel as to put such a good wee dog as that into the canal, they didn't deserve to get keeping it. Willie, however, insisted on keeping his promise to his wife. He put on his cap, took the dog in his arms, and, pausing at the door to say he wasn't taking anybody with him, he added, ' Well, Serah, Ah'm away.'

' Well, don't be long,' she retorted.

He looked at her, a twinkle in his eye. ' Whi'd'ye mean ? '

' Oh, nothing. Just—well—you don't need to go awful far,' adding, as a sop to her pride, ' I've got a lot for you to do in the house.'

He went out, returning five minutes later saying that the dog's snout had been so continuously poking into his leg that he couldn't go any distance Everybody was delighted. As for Sarah, she filled up the big tub that had been so often used to bath her children. ' I'll look out an old towel,' she said.

Having been washed, with some difficulty, the dog was found to be mostly a brindle Cairn. Then followed quite an argument over what the animal was to be called. Willie wanted it to be 'Lassie'; Polly's choice was 'Dinky'; Matt's 'Winky,' because of the drooping ear which he insisted was a doggy wink; Peter howled with rage because nobody thought much of his suggestion which was 'Beastie'; Sarah and Maisie declared jointly that 'Bessie' was as good a name as any. The matter had finally to be settled with the aid of Willie's bowler hat, Maisie drawing the lots. Willie's piece of paper came out first, so 'Lassie' it was.

There was, two days later, an abortive attempt on the part of the children to christen the dog, an episode of which Sarah was so ashamed that it had better be passed over quickly.

A notice appeared in the sweetie-shop window, saying, 'Found—a dog. If not claimed before Saturday will be kept. W. McFlannel, 122 Partick Road.' Willie, for his part, had an uneasy feeling that there was something irregular in the whole proceedings, and he shared the family's fear that, before Saturday, Lassie's owner would turn up. It was, for some reason or other, a great relief to everyone when, the following Saturday, Willie bought a licence as well as a dog-collar with his name and address on it. Lassie was theirs. At least, she was everybody's as long as she behaved herself. On other occasions she was Willie's.

CHAPTER 4

THIRTY SHILLINGS A MONTH

Two years went by, years in which Maisie had the whooping cough, Peter the measles, Lassie had learned to roll over, to give a paw, to carry slippers and newspapers ; Matt had passed into the secondary school, Sarah had frequent differences of opinion with Mrs. McTweed, Willie had raised his account in the savings bank to three figures in the £ column, and Polly had attained her fourteenth year.

'I don't want to stay on at the school,' the girl protested. 'I want to go out to work.'

Sarah was disappointed and showed it. 'Well, you'll just have to learn shorthand and typing.'

'I don't want to be a typist. I want to serve in a shop.'

'What ! after you getting a Higher Grade education !'

'I never wanted a Higher Grade education !'

'Well, you're not going to work in any shop. That's flat !'

'But I don't want to work in an office. I want to work some place cheery !'

'You want !—you want !' jeered Sarah. 'You'll do what you're told, my girl !'

But Polly proving adamant on the subject of shorthand and typing lessons, a compromise was made, and every evening the 'Situations Vacant' column was small-tooth-combed for advertisers anxious for an office girl. At last the very thing Sarah was looking for turned up, and she and Polly got down to the task of composing a letter of application.

'You'd better put down your age first,' advised Sarah, 'and don't forget to use the word " Re." It sounds real businesslike. Then you'll have to say something about your education. Tell them that you've had Science and Mathematics and French and Latin and—what else ?'

Polly hesitated, and Willie from behind his newspaper interjected, 'Two quarters at the pianna.'

'Shsh !' ordered Sarah, uncertain as to whether or not her
husband was laughing at her. 'How are you going to put all
that down, Polly ?'

'Ugh,' exclaimed the girl, 'I'll just say I was educated at
Partick Higher Grade.'

To Sarah, however, the full list of those subjects of which
she herself had been brought up in ignorance was the most
important item in her daughter's equipment, so down went
the whole impressive list—Science, Mathematics, French, and
Latin.

'What about English ?' inquired Polly.

'Oh, don't bother about that. Everybody speaks English !'

'Except Daddy,' whispered Polly.

Willie, having missed the whisper, said, 'Don't forget tae
tell them ye had drawin' lessons, an' that ye'll be able tae draw a
fat salary.' He laughed at his own wit, but not finding his
amusement shared he returned to his newspaper.

'What now ?' asked Sarah. 'D'you not think you should
say something about your appearance ?' She was very proud
that Polly had taken after her side of the house.

The girl fidgeted. She was beginning to realize that a few
lessons on the science of applying for a job would have been of
more service to her than chemistry, but the letter was completed
at last, and for the next day or two Sarah watched the postman's
movements closely. When, on the third morning, a card
was pushed through the door, she rushed to the bedroom,
calling :

'Polly ! Polly ! Waken up ! Here's a postcard for you.
And from a Sheriff Officer, no less !'

The girl, aching with sleep, took the card and read : 'With
reference to your application, please call here at 2 p.m. to-morrow
(Thursday).' She blinked. So it had come at last ! Oh well,
maybe they wouldn't like her at the interview.

'Now get up, there's a good girl,' pleaded Sarah. 'You'll
take a bath before you go and you can put on your Sunday

clothes. My, you're the lucky girl ! Fancy getting the chance to work in a Sheriff Officer's ! '

It was only the force of her mother's enthusiasm which ultimately got Polly out of the house in time, and for the rest of the afternoon Sarah was in a fever of excitement. Would Polly get the job ? Had she remembered to clean her teeth ? It would be simply wonderful if she got the job ! Sheriff Officer ! My word—what would Mrs. M'Cotton say when she heard it ! The hours dragged by and still Polly didn't return. By the time Willie came home from his work Sarah was in a state of alarm and despondency.

' Oh, Willie,' she wailed, ' what d'you think's happened to her ? '

' She's jumped intae the canawl ! ' suggested Willie callously. ' Ye kent fine she never wanted tae work in an office ! '

Just when Sarah was thinking of sending Matt for the police, Polly arrived.

' Where have you been ? ' demanded Sarah, her voice shrill with anxiety not yet allayed.

' Working,' replied the girl calmly. ' He asked me to start right away.'

' You got the job, then ? ' exclaimed Sarah ecstatically.

' Uhha.'

' In a Sheriff Officer's ! My-my ! '

' What's he like ? ' demanded Matt.

' I'll tell you when I've had my tea.'

Immediately a plateful of ham and egg was laid before her, while her mother stood by, clasping and unclasping her hands in an orgy of admiration.

' Wis it yer Science an' Latin an' stuff that did the trick ? ' asked her father.

' No. He liked my writing ! '

Sarah, however, was beyond the reach of innuendo. ' What kind of man is he ? ' she asked. ' Does he wear a black gown and one of thon white curly wigs ? '

Polly laughed. ' No. He's just an ordinary man—like Daddy. He even speaks like Daddy.'

' Ugh away ! ' jerked out Matt. ' I always thought sheriffs were two-gun men with horses and spurs and big boots, that went about saying, " Stick 'em up, ya rattlesnake ! " '

The quotation, as well as the manner of its delivery, called forth a torrent of abuse from his mother, ending up with, ' What d'you mean, reading that trash when I've told you so often not to ! Have you got one of those books in the house just now ? '

Matt looked uncomfortable. So did his father, who was at the moment sitting on a copy of *Ridin' West* which he had filched from beneath Matt's Algebra book. Polly, feeling that the centre of interest had passed from her, brought back everyone's attention by saying :

' I was at the Court this afternoon.'

' You what ! ' exclaimed Sarah. ' What were you doing there ? '

' I was taking some summonses to the Small Debt Office.'

' My word ! Wait till I tell Mrs. M'Cotton ! She'll be mad when she hears it—and her Dick just a common workman.'

' Like yer ain man ! ' said Willie quietly.

Sarah ignored him. Instead she feasted her eyes on her daughter—her clever, successful Polly. Fancy her getting a job in a Sheriff Officer's and going to the Court. What next ! ' Hurry up with your tea, Polly,' she urged. ' I want to run across to Mrs. M'Cotton. I'm asking her and Mr. M'Cotton up for tea next week with the McLeathers.'

' Whit's that ? ' demanded Willie. ' This is the first Ah've heard o't ! '

' Well, you've got to hear everything for the first time some time ! '

Oh, life was just grand ! Willie was on full time again and his foreman wasn't keeping at all well ; Maisie was dux of her class ; Matt was something or other in the school football team ; wee Peter would be going to school next week (she certainly would miss the wee chap toddling about the house, but there was always Lassie, the best wee dog in the world, and weren't they the lucky people to have her !) ; it was a pity about Maisie's cold, but a day or two in bed would soon put her right ; and here was Polly with this grand job. My-oh-my! Where would they end, with all this success!

'How much are you getting a week, Polly?' she asked rather belatedly.

'Thirty shillings a month!' was the reply.

'A month!' echoed Sarah. Fancy that now! If that wasn't a step up in the social scale, what was! A monthly salary instead of a vulgar weekly wage, such as Dick M'Cotton got. Mrs. M'Cotton wouldn't half be green with envy. Sarah scuttled around, tidying everything and everyone. She must get away soon, but first of all she must see that Maisie, lying there so patiently in the bedroom, was comfortable. She put on her hat and coat and ran into the bedroom.

'My throat's awful sore,' complained the child.

Sarah gaped at her, wide-eyed. There was something queer-looking about her; she was different from what she had been an hour before. What was wrong? It couldn't be the measles—she had had that when she was three.

'Let me see your tongue, hen.'

Maisie, with difficulty, pushed out a filthy tongue, then began to cry, her breath wheezing and gulping.

'Daddy!' called Sarah, and there was that in her tone that fetched Willie instantaneously. Following his wife's frightened look he bent over the child, placing his hand on her brow. The way he pursed up his lips as he felt its heat made Sarah conscious of an odd sensation in the backs of her legs. Whatever was the matter?

'D'you think it—it's just an awful bad cold?' she whispered. 'She says her throat's sore.'

Willie shook his head. 'Ah think ye'd better get the doctor jist tae make sure.'

Since she was all dressed for outdoors, Sarah herself hurried out to the surgery round the corner. The doctor was out, but he would get the message all right, the dispenser assured her. Oh dear! Wee Maisie! Should she poultice her, she wondered, as she ran back home. She found Willie still by the bedside. There seemed to be some change for the worse even in that short time.

'Oh, Willie,' she moaned. 'What do you think it is? Can you not think of something to help her?'

Willie, troubled, could only reach out an awkward hand and clasp hers. She leaned towards him. He was the stupidest, clumsiest, commonest of men, but at a time like this she wanted no-one else. A pat from his big rough hand was worth all the empty words of other women's husbands.

'D'you think it's the fever?'

'Ah'm no' sure, lass. Maybe it's dip'theria.'

Oh dear-dear! Poor wee Maisie! Would they let her look after her at home? Not likely, seeing there were the others to think about. Ah! The others! If this was dip'theria, what about Polly's swell job if she had to stay off her work till the house was fumigated? And what about Matt? Matt—who was so elated over playing this big match to-morrow. The well of Sarah's woe filled up and overflowed in tears.

'Don't greet, lass!' said Willie. 'She'll be a'right. There's the bell! That'll be the doctor.' As his wife turned from him, a sudden thought occurred to the man. Brushing his hand across his eyes he said, 'Heh, Serah. Cheer up. Ye never died a winter yet.'

With a blink of courage Sarah opened the door.

Yes, it was diphtheria all right. The rest of the household were examined and told to take precautions. Within an hour it was all over—the ambulance at the close, with the crowd of gaping children holding their noses against infection; the blanket-wrapped bundle that was Maisie being carried out; the putting out of five cups and saucers instead of six for supper; the tears; the garglings. It was all over. However were they going to put in all those weeks that must elapse before Maisie came home again? Polly's job didn't seem quite so wonderful now—all the same it was good that she wouldn't need to stay off her work; Matt would get to his football match all right, too. Sarah dried her tears. There couldn't be any thought now of inviting the M'Cottons and the McLeathers for tea next week—but maybe, after Maisie was better a bit, they could come. . . .

CHAPTER 5

THE CLANS HAVE TEA

IT was Wednesday afternoon, three weeks later. Maisie was definitely better, and the M'Cottons and the McLeathers were coming for tea. Sarah was setting the table when Peter arrived home from school ; coming back into the kitchen after opening the door for the boy, she sniffed.

'There's an awful funny smell in here. Do you feel it, son ? ' she asked.

Peter sniffed. ' Naw ! ' he said.

' Don't say " naw " ! How often have I to tell you ? '

' My daddy says " naw." '

' But you don't want to grow up to speak like your daddy, do you ? '

' Ay ! '

' There you go again ! ' But the odd smell was more disturbing than Peter's speech. Sarah sniffed again. ' Here—that's a *terrible* smell ! It's coming from over by the fire. I wonder if there's something in the oven—— '

At that Peter yelped. ' Oh, my bools, my bools ! ' He ran to the oven so excitedly that Lassie began to bark.

' What bools ? ' demanded his mother, opening the oven door ; then, as the sorry spectacle of a dripping, sticky mess pouring from one of the shelves met her gaze, she turned on Peter. ' You wee rascal, you ! Is that tar ? '

' Ay. I got some off the road at dinner-time, and I made it into bools and I put them into the oven to harden.'

' To harden ! Of all the senseless notions ! Just look at the mess ! To say nothing of the smell—and all these folk coming for tea. I'll give you a hammering for that, you stupid wee torment, you ! ' She scraped at the tar with an old knife, uncomfortably certain that she would never get it off in time. Just then the doorbell rang and she sent Peter off to find out who

47

it was. She was absorbed in the task of scraping when her husband poked her in the back. Turning round she snapped, 'Oh, it's you, is it!'

'Ay. Who wis ye expeckin'?'

'Don't be silly. Just look at this mess your precious Peter has made trying to make bools with tar! As if I hadn't enough to do with all those folk coming for their tea, and me not near ready yet!'

Willie took off his jacket. 'See here—Ah'll dae that fur ye!'

'No, you won't! It would be more like the thing if you gave that brat a leathering for making such a mess. Away you go and clean yourself as fast as you can, and don't be any longer in that sink than you can help.'

'Ah'm no' goin' intae the sink. Ah jist want tae wash ma haunds an' face.'

'Ugh, don't try to be funny, and me in such a habble. *Hurry!* I've got all your clean things laid out there. And keep out of my road, for I'm as cross as two sticks.'

'Ach, cheer up! Ye never died a winter yet. Gie's a wee cheeper.'

Sarah wrenched herself out of her husband's affectionate grasp. 'Oh, stop your nonsense. Are you drunk, or what? Here, let me go!'

But Willie was determined. 'Come on, Serah. Jist a wee yin!'

'Ugh, Willie, don't aggravate me. What do you want a kiss for at such a daft-like time?'

'Never mind. Ah'll tell ye efter Ah get ma cheeper.'

'Let me go!' She tore herself free. What was the matter with the man? There was a hilarious glint in his eye that she hadn't seen since Maisie had gone to hospital. Why wasn't he making his usual protests about folk being invited for tea? 'I've no time to waste!' she told him. 'Away you go and wash yourself and let me get on with the setting of the table.' She escaped with the oven shelf, flinging it into the coal-bunker. Was the smell away yet?

For a few minutes nothing was heard but the rattle of crockery and the rush of water as Willie washed himself at the sink. ' Where's a' the faimly the night ? ' he queried at last.

' Polly's working late. It's a right nuisance, so it is, and me needing her help so much.'

' Is Matt no' hame f'ae the school yet ? '

' He's at a football match. I'm sure you've heard plenty about it.'

' Ach, Ah forgot.'

' You haven't forgotten, have you, that wee Maisie's in the hospital with dip'theria ? '

' Ah have nut. Puir wee sowl. Ah hope they're bein' guid tae 'er.'

Sarah, however, was too thrang to be troubled with a problem over which she had already expended so much mental energy. ' Come on,' she ordered. ' Are you not near finished in that sink yet ? '

' Ah'm comin', Ah'm comin',' he assured her, adding, ' Ehm, Ah say, Serah—Ah hope ye're no' expeckin' me tae ladle oot fish the night. Ye mind whit happened the last time we had veesitors.'

' Fine I mind. But it's not fish ! I don't want Mrs. M'Cotton to know we can't afford fish knives and forks. It's boiled bacon, and for goodness' sake don't start telling thon story again.'

Willie dried himself thoughtfully. ' Whit story ? Oh, thon yin aboot the funeral ? Ach, there's nothin' in thon ! '

' Well, I don't like it. And another thing—don't say, " Eat up, we're in the Co," or " The mair ye eat the bigger the dividend." It's awful common.'

' Anythin' else Ah've tae don't ? '

' Plenty, but I suppose it's no use speaking. Is it any use asking you not to talk politics ? '

' Ma conscience, Serah, what *are* we tae talk aboot ? Whether we should hae wur troosers slashed up the sides, or—or whether galluses should match the colour o' wur eyes ? '

' That's right—make a fool of me ! ' Sarah, slicing the bread, blinked back a tear of vexation.

' Puir Serah—ye've an awful job bringin' up yer man ! '

' There's one thing I've given up hope of anyway.'

' Whit's that ? Makin' me use a napkin right ? '

' Mphm.'

' Well, whit's a man tae dae wi' the thing ? If 'e spreads it on the lap he hasnae got, it slides ontae the fluir an' gets scuffed. When Ah dribble, Ah dribble ontae ma tie an' ma vest, an' inside ma collar's the only place fur the thing. Ach, it's nothin' but a palaver onywey.' Willie, with the freedom of his class, changed his clothes as he spoke, not heeding Peter who was lying on the floor playing with Lassie.

' Well, if I didn't put down napkins that woman M'Cotton would think I hadn't any. Here, Peter ! Come and eat this ! '

' Whit's that ? ' asked Willie, peering at a plateful of bread and jam. ' Whit's the idea ? '

Peter, from the floor, declared that he wasn't hungry, at any rate not bread-hungry.

' You'll just sit down there and eat the lot before the folk come ! ' commanded his mother. ' I don't want you to give me a showing up eating all the French cakes. Come on, now, or I'll take my hand off your face, you wee rascal ! That smell's never away yet ! '

Peter moved with reluctance towards the sink while his mother examined the table. Was everything there ? She must remember to see that the handbasin in the bathroom was clean. Ah—there was the doorbell.

' Now, Peter ! ' whispered Sarah fiercely as she took off her overall. ' Not one word out of your head about the folk being invited here to-night to see the new bedroom suite ! Mind ! '

It was, of course, the M'Cottons—ten minutes before they were due, but Willie was ready to receive Mr. M'Cotton at the parlour fireplace, while Sarah conducted Mrs. M'Cotton to the bedroom where she treated the new suite with elaborate unconcern—treatment that was copied by her visitor. The McLeathers, on the other hand, were twenty minutes late, and the intervening half-hour put a heavy strain on the host and hostess. Lassie was eventually called in to go through her tricks for the benefit of the visitors, but Mrs. M'Cotton, being of the type that always knows a trickier dog, was not impressed. The McLeathers were hailed with enthusiasm by Sarah.

Willie managed to negotiate with tolerable ease all the pitfalls of etiquette about which he had been warned ; all the same the relief in his voice was obvious when, at the end of the meal, he said :

'Well, chaps, if that's wur tea, we've had it, as the poet says.' Giving a jerk of his head to the two gentlemen visitors, he added, 'Come on ben the hoose. The ladies'll clear up.'

'The ladies'll do nothing of the kind !' retorted Sarah. 'I'll manage fine myself. I'll just put the dishes in the sink and Polly can help me when she comes home.'

'Away wi'ye !' said Mrs. McLeather, who, unlike Mrs. M'Cotton, had no social pretensions. 'We'll give you a hand.'

'Oh, certainly !' said Mrs. M'Cotton without noticeable fervour.

'You clear away the bread and things, Mrs. McFlannel, and Mrs. M'Cotton an' me'll wash the dishes,' suggested Mrs. McLeather.

The men, untrammelled by any responsibility towards the cleaning of the dishes they had dirtied, passed in a lordly procession through the doorway towards the parlour. As they went, Willie's voice drifted back to the kitchen, 'Did ye ever hear the story aboot the auld man an' the boiled bacon ? '

'My !' exclaimed Sarah as the parlour door banged, 'that man of mine'll be the death of me yet. I don't know how often I've asked him to stop telling that story ! '

'What is it about anyway ? ' asked Mrs. M'Cotton, taking off her wristlet watch and depositing it in a prominent place.

'Ugh, it's that silly I'm near ashamed to repeat it. It's supposed to be an old man that's dying and his wife asks him if there's anything he'd like, and he says, " Ah'd jist like a wee tait o' thon boiled bacon," and she says, " Ye cannae get that—it's fur yer funeral." '

Mrs. McLeather nodded in grim appreciation, not of the story but of Sarah's discomfiture. 'My man's the same,' she sympathized. 'He's got one he's awful fond of—something the same—about an Aberdonian that's dying, and his wife says to him, "I've to run oot a wee messagie, Dod. If ye feel yersel' slippin' awa' afore I win back jist blah oot the cannle!" And d'you know, if I've asked him once, I've asked him dozens of times not to tell that story, but it's no use.'

'Ugh—men are all the same,' complained Sarah.

Mrs. M'Cotton felt it was time for her to show her superiority. 'Well, Eh must say, meh husband is *most* attentive to *all* Eh say.'

Ignoring the observation, Mrs. McLeather asked if Mrs. M'Cotton would wash or dry.

'Oh, perhaps you'd better wash,' was the reply. 'Meh frock's a new one and it was frehtfully expensive. Eh got it in Sauchiehall Street, you know. Eh'd hate to——'

'Here!' said Sarah, 'I've got aprons for you both, but I can easy manage the dishes myself.'

Mrs. M'Cotton accepted the apron, but Mrs. McLeather, anxious to offset the gentility of her fellow-visitor, declined it with a few pointed remarks, which made Sarah feel uncomfortable. Mrs. McLeather was a decent soul, thought Sarah, but she shouldn't say those things. What if Mrs. M'Cotton took offence? But that lady, wrapped in the imperviousness of her own conceit, had apparently noticed nothing. As she dried the dishes daintily, she said:

'You know, Mrs. McFlehnnel, Eh think it's wonderful of you letting strangers wash your dishes. Eh know Eh wouldn't. Of course, mehn are real china!'

The cat, thought Sarah. Oh well, there was only one way to deal with that. 'Oh, that's all right!' she said blithely. 'These aren't my best things. I keep them for special friends.'

'Is that so? Oh, Eh must tell you about a party of very special friends Eh had for supper last night——'

At that moment there was a gust of laughter heard blowing from the parlour. 'My!' said Mrs. McLeather, with a regrettable lack of interest in Mrs. M'Cotton's very special supperparty. 'These men are fairly enjoying themselves.'

But Mrs. M'Cotton ignored the interruption. ' Eh had the McRubbers—awf'lly nice people they are—they have a villa out at Jordanhill. Do you know them ? '

' No, I don't,' said Mrs. McLeather ungraciously. ' The only folk I know that live in a villa stay out at Mosspark ! '

Mrs. M'Cotton snorted with contempt. ' Oh, Mosspark ! ' She allowed her contempt to sink in, then went on : ' And Eh had the McPlushes—they're awf'lly nice people too—Eh wonder if you know them—they live in Hyndland—they've a beautiful fleht with an interior grate in the kitchen.'

The burst of laughter which at that moment reached them from the parlour seemed directed in derision towards Mrs. M'Cotton's last remark, but Mrs. McLeather missed the point, so keen was she to say :

' Ugh, what's the good of having an interior grate in the kitchen as long as you've got a coal-bunker and clothes-pulleys and a sink and all ? To say nothing of the bed-place ! '

' Oh, but you should see how splendidly the McPlushes have got their kitchen done up ! ' exclaimed Mrs. M'Cotton—' just like a dining-room ! They've got a wooden sort of cover for the sink, and Mrs. McPlush has made the cutest curtain for the gas cooker. She even keeps a plant on it ! '

Mrs. McLeather, however, remained unmoved. ' She must be real vexed when she has to fry a kipper,' was her retort.

Unheedingly, Mrs. M'Cotton continued : ' And of course they haven't got a bed in the bed-place. The McPlushes are really superior people—they'd never dream of having a bed in the kitchen ! '

Sarah intercepted a meaning look at that corner of her kitchen where Willie and she slept, but she was content to leave Mrs. McLeather to deal with the situation.

' Just fancy that, now ! ' was that lady's bored comment. ' Oh, Mrs. McFlannel, is that everything ? ' The dishes were washed but, owing to Mrs. M'Cotton's interest in her own affairs, they were not yet dried. Sarah, sweeping the tablecloth with the brush-and-crumb tray she had bought specially for the occasion, said that it was, and Mrs. McLeather seized an extra dish-towel and gave all her attention to the drying of the dishes, while Mrs. M'Cotton continued her monologue about some more of her acquaintances whom she claimed as lifelong friends. At length, however, thanks to Mrs. McLeather, the job was done, and as a fresh gale of laughter was blown from the other end of the house, Sarah said :

' Come on away ben and hear what all the noise is about ! '

Mrs. M'Cotton protested that she had not completed her catalogue of social conquests, but her hostess was adamant, and the three of them moved towards the parlour. As the door was flung open, there was a sudden lull in the laughter and a noticeable lowering of the convivial temperature. After seats had been found for everybody, Willie said meditatively, as if to fill the conversational gap, ' Well. . . .'

' Ah,' replied Mr. M'Cotton, to which Mr. McLeather retorted, ' Mphm.'

' Come on,' urged Sarah. ' Tell us what you were laughing at.'

' We've been having wonderful weather,' declared Mr. M'Cotton, who suddenly realizing that he had made this statement earlier in the evening while awaiting the arrival of the McLeathers decided to vary it by adding, ' for this time of the year, anyway.'

Willie entered into the spirit of the thing and agreed enthusiastically ; as for Mr. McLeather, he eased his collar from his neck and pronounced that hot weather like this couldn't last long. Then Willie, sensing that Sarah was about to renew the attack, defended himself forehanded by asking where wee Peter was.

' Yes, but——' interposed Sarah.

The men huddled together spiritually. ' He came in here along with us,' said Mr. McLeather.

Mr. M'Cotton reached a long arm down the back of the sofa. ' Here's Peter ! ' he announced. ' Come on out and show yourself, son.'

' Did you tell yon story about the candle ? ' demanded Mrs. McLeather of her husband, who, however, was by this time too intent on searching his pockets for a suitably small coin with which to reward Peter for reciting to the company to reply. Peter proved a broken reed, though, for he insisted that Lassie required exercise—a pretext that even his father could not ignore. He left the room as Mrs. M'Cotton asked :

' How is Polly getting on at her work, Mrs. McFlannel ? She'll be serving in a shop, I suppose ? '

Sarah was indignant. ' She is not ! She's in a Sheriff Officer's office. I told you. She goes to the Court, too ! '

' How nice ! And how about Matt ? Is he going to be a workman like his father ? '

' Oh, no,' said Sarah with bashful grandiloquence, ' Matt wants to be a doctor.'

' Is that so ? Isn't it odd the notions they take when they're young ? Our Dick wanted to be a Member of Parliament.'

Sarah smiled pityingly. ' And here he's gone into the black squad after all.'

Mrs. M'Cotton brushed aside the pity. ' Oh well, of course, he's got to serve his apprenticeship. He's going to be a draughts-man, you know.'

The balloon of Sarah's superiority being thus rudely pricked, she tried to catch what Mr. M'Cotton was whispering that the other two men were so eager to hear, but as she had no success there was nothing else for it but to revert to Mrs. M'Cotton, who seemed determined to ignore the other visitor. ' I'm fairly missing wee Maisie,' said Sarah. ' When she comes out the hospital, I think I'll take her down to Millport for a wee holiday.' She spoke softly, lest Willie should hear and make voluble protest, the idea not having occurred to her until this moment.

' Oh, Millport ! ' exclaimed Mrs. M'Cotton with a flick of her hand. ' Millport is so common. In fect, all the Clyde resorts are getting quate impossible. Our friends the McDruggits —that's the awf'lly nice people Eh was telling you about who live out at Bearsden—they're talking about going to Crail, and they're most anxious that we should go too.'

' Oh ? Is Mr. McDruggit — ehm — a clerk, like Mr. M'Cotton ? '

' Oh, no ! He's in business for himself.'

' Is that so ? What kind of business is it ? '

' Eh—really—couldn't say——'

' He keeps a fish-and-chip shop in the Maryhill Road,' interjected Mr. M'Cotton, with so much spite that it was obvious he didn't share his wife's enthusiasm for their friends ; after that the conversation sagged again, until one of the men had the inspired idea of introducing the subject of politics and that kept the men content—although no observer would have suspected it from their heated disagreements—for the rest of the evening. The women, for their part, waged a battle that was far more real in spite of their seemingly cool demeanour. Mrs. M'Cotton continued to carry the banner of her boastfulness into the camp of her two enemies, who seemed to have a tacit ability to ignore the flaunting of the banner. She finally raised herself in the saddle of her pride and proclaimed that she and her husband were thinking of moving into one of the new houses.

' You mean—a Scheme house ? ' inquired Mrs. McLeather.

' Good gracious, no ! Either a bungalow or a semi-detached villa. We'll have to buy, of course.'

' Oh ? So much down and the rest up ? ' was Mrs. McLeather's comment.

Sarah left the two of them to it and went to the kitchen for the bowlful of fruit, which she passed round, along with plates and knives. The gesture was generally accepted as being a hint that the evening's entertainment was now concluded. Half an hour later they were all standing in the small lobby saying good-night to one another with protestations of mutual enjoyment.

' We've had a grand time,' insisted Mrs. McLeather.

' And so have we,' added Sarah.

' You'll all have to come and see us as soon as we get settled in our new house,' exclaimed Mrs. M'Cotton from half-way down the stair.

' Yes. Yes. Good-night. Good-night.'

The door was closed at length. ' Thank goodness that's over,' sighed Sarah.

'But ye're jist new-done sayin' ye enjoyed yersel',' protested Willie.

'Ugh ! My, but that woman M'Cotton fairly rubs me the wrong way, blowing away there about her *awf'lly* nice friends, and her *awf'lly* expensive clothes, and her *awf'lly* superior furniture !'

'Cheer up, Serah——'

'I know. I never died a winter yet.'

'Naw, Ah wisnae gonnae say that this time. Ah wis jist—ehm—wantin' tae tell ye somethin'.'

'What ?'

'Ye'll can crow over Mrs. M'Cotton the next time ye see her.'

'How ? Don't tantalize me, Willie.'

'Ah got somethin' the day—somethin' ye've been greinin' efter for a long time.'

Sarah searched her husband's face. 'Not your hat !' she exclaimed. 'Have they given you the foreman's hat at last ?'

Willie nodded. 'Ay. Ye'll be happy noo ! Nothin' left tae wish fur. Eh ?'

'My, but you're the limit ! Why could you not have told me that whenever you came in ?'

'Ah wanted tae, but ye widnae let me.'

'I never did !'

'D'ye no' mind ye widnae gie me a wee cheeper when Ah asked ye ?'

'Ugh ! You and your cheepers ! I wish you had told me, so's I could've held up my head to that woman M'Cotton.'

'Are ye no' even gonnae congratulate me ?'

His tone was so wistful that she could only smack him playfully in the darkness of the lobby, and, lest he should imagine she was getting sentimental, she led the way into the lighted kitchen. After a while, the family all in bed, she sidled up to him with a look in her eyes like that of a girl of sixteen. 'Willie !' she said wheedlingly.

'Ay ? Whit noo ?' The man knew the signs.

'What do you say to going out on Saturday to see these

new bungalows and semi-detached villas they're building. I don't mean the Corporation kind, I mean the kind you buy up.'

Willie looked at her, shaking his head. ' Ye're a great wee wumman, Serah. But there's nothin' doin'. D'ye hear? Nothin' doin'! Ma name's no' M'Cotton.'

CHAPTER 6

WANTED—ANOTHER HOUSE

SARAH couldn't sleep. To-morrow would see the start of the spring cleaning. Should she shift the piano? Or the sideboard? Supposing she put the sofa in front of the fireplace and brought one of the easy-chairs into the kitchen? . . . The kitchen? Maybe she would have been better to have got a painter in to whitewash the kitchen ceiling. As for the shelves! How on earth had her mother managed to bring up seven children, and all those dishes on the kitchen shelves to keep clean? For a few minutes Sarah allowed her thoughts to roam around the memory of her mother's trials, then she remembered her own. Ah—those kitchen shelves! How many times would this be that she had spring-cleaned this house? Polly was what—twelve when they flitted in. She was seventeen now, and beginning to giggle at the boys and point out how much nicer other people's houses were than her own home. Well, if she, Sarah, had had her way, they would have left Partick Road long ago, but Willie had jumped on her every time she mentioned the subject. Ach—he was a right stick-in-the-mud. Sarah rolled over on her other side and began mentally to rearrange the parlour furniture all over again. She got to sleep eventually.

About eleven o'clock the following forenoon there was a terrific peal on the doorbell. Sarah, high up on the steps, tut-tutted; while she was still in the act of climbing down, the bell rang again. She flung open the door in a flurry of indignation. Mrs. McTweed was just about to pull the bell for the third time.

'Here,' shrieked the visitor. 'Whit'd'ye mean keepin' me staunin' here fur—kiddin' on ye werenae in!'

'I wasn't kidding on anything! I was at the top of my steps doing my shelves, and if I've had to come down once I've had to come down a dozen times. First it was——'

Mrs. McTweed interrupted her. 'Ah don't care a tuppeny

59

ticket who it wis. Whit Ah want tae know is—whit did you steal ma doormat fur ? '

' I never touched your doormat ! '

' Well, whit's it daein' at your door ? Ah'm sayin' whit's it daein' at your door ? ' Mrs. McTweed demanded in duplicate, as was her wont, and pointing an accusing finger in the direction of her feet.

Sarah gaped at the evidence. Right enough, that wasn't her own doormat that was lying there. ' I don't know,' she began timidly, but spunked up to add, ' If you think I would stoop to touch your scuddy wee mat——'

' It's nothin' o' the kind a scuddy wee mat—it's as guid as yours, if no' better. Ah'm jist away tae the Polis Office, fur Ah'm sick tae daith o' the hale McFlannel fam'ly. The things Ah've suffered ! Ah'm sayin' the things Ah've suffered.' She glanced upwards as though to implore supernatural sympathy. None being forthcoming, Sarah took the opportunity to ask :

' But where's *my* mat ? Is it at your door ? '

' It is not ! If you think——'

At that moment Sarah spied her mat lying in front of the opposite door. She pounced on it, saying, ' Here's mine. It's been some of the children playing themselves.'

' Playin' theirsel's ! ' Once again Mrs. McTweed's eyes were uplifted. ' Ah wish Ah had the haud o' them ! Tyin' doorbells tae door haunles, an' pittin' squeebs in the keyholes, an' stuffin' the washin'-hoose chimney, an' settin' fire tae the ashpits, an' playin' fitba' in the back coorts, an'—an' dear kens a' whit ! '

Sarah tried to defend her offspring, but the fountain of her neighbour's eloquence was not yet dried up.

' The place hasnae been fit tae live in since youse McFlannels flitted in—an' you ca' it " playin' theirsel's " ! They're nothin' but a gang o' young hooligans ! '

' They're no worse than other folk's children, and they're a sight better than a cat,' said Sarah, a remark which started off a discussion about the relative merits of Mrs. McTweed's cat and the McFlannels' dog, a discussion that became so intimate and slanderous to the animals concerned that we had better turn our heads away, bringing them back again at the point where Sarah said :

'Well, now that you know I didn't steal your old doormat, what about taking your foot off my doorstep and letting me get on with my work ? '

'Work ? ' retorted Mrs. McTweed. 'Ah'm surprised to hear ye've ony to do. Ye've gi'en yersel' sich airs since yer man wis made a foreman that it's a wunner ye havenae a butler or some-body tae make the beds fur ye an' take doon yer ashes.'

Sarah retreated into her house. 'Here—that's enough,' she warned.

'Oh naw, it's no'. Ah'm sayin' it's no' ! Ah've been ettlin' fur months tae gie you a bit o' ma mind, an' ye're gonnae get it. It's high time somebody wis tellin' ye whitna laughin' stock ye are ! Dressin' yersel' up in yer new hat an' coat, an' trippin' doon tae the midden wi' yer rubbidge tied up in a parcel ! '

'Folk should mind their own business ! ' put in Sarah as Mrs. McTweed paused to draw her breath.

'Huh ! ' went on Mrs. McTweed, refreshed, 'gettin' a wumman tae wash the stairs fur ye. An' yer pan-loaf talk ! "Good-marning, Mrs. McTweed," says you, "fehn weather we're heving for this tehm of the year ! " '

Sarah, squirming, felt like kicking the trespassing foot from her doorstep. 'Oh, for goodness' sake, shut up ! ' she blurted out.

'Oh, but Ah'm no' near dune yet ! Ye should hear whit folk are sayin' aboot you no' wearin' a dust-cap when yer hair's new waved.'

'Will you please take your foot off my doorstep ? '

'Wait yer hurry, Ah'm sayin' wait yer hurry ! Ah'm no' budgin' till Ah've had ma say. The things Ah've suffered offa youse McFlannels ! Whit between yer man ham-ham-hammerin' an' the weans' feet clat-clat-clatterin'——'

Sarah had had enough—more than enough. In any case there was someone coming up the stairs. She drew in a big breath and said, 'Well, you'll not have very long to suffer it now.'

'Oh !' Mrs. McTweed was taken aback and showed it. 'Are yez flittin'? Whaur tae?'

'That's *my* business !' retorted Sarah rather evasively. 'I'll give you another chance to take your foot away *and* your old doormat——'

'Oh, jist a meenit. Ah'm sayin' jist a meenit. Are yez flittin' tae a New Hoose?'

The stair climber came into view and Sarah saw with delight that it was her friend Mrs. McLeather. 'Excuse me,' she said with great dignity to the gaping woman on the doormat. 'Here's somebody wanting to see me.'

Grabbing Mrs. McLeather with an effusiveness that surprised that lady, she said, 'Come away in. I'm awful pleased to see you.' In a moment the door was shut and they were in the kitchen, and Mrs. McTweed was left in undisputed possession of her doormat.

'I'm in a terrible habble,' began Sarah, as she shifted steps, chairs, brushes, pails, in order to give Mrs. McLeather a seat. 'I'm in the middle of my spring cleaning.'

'I thought I heard you say something about a flitting when I was coming up the stair. You never told me.' There was a suggestion of huffiness in Mrs. McLeather's tones.

'I didn't know myself until two minutes ago !' protested Sarah. 'Did you hear what that bizzum was saying to me?'

'Some of it. She's a tartar, that one. I don't know how you've stood her so long.'

'Neither do I. But my mind's made up this time. That's the worst of a tenement—you've no liberty. Did you hear what she said about my pan-loaf talk?'

'No. She was just ham-ham-hammerin' when I came up the stair.'

Self-consciously Sarah asked, 'Do *you* think I talk pan loaf?'

'I never noticed it. You're not as bad as Mrs. M'Cotton anyway.'

In self-defence Sarah went on : 'It's not that I want to—to let-on I'm better than other folk. It's just—I don't want my family to grow up and feel ashamed of their mother.'

62

' Don't you worry ! ' advised Mrs. McLeather with surprising
sagacity, ' they'd feel ashamed of you if you were a duchess. It's
a way families have.'

' I suppose it is.' Mournfully, Sarah filled up the kettle and
lit the gas-ring. ' What's worrying me now is—how I'll get
Willie to agree to flit. He always gets into such a rage every
time I speak about it, that of late I've said nothing, and he'll be
thinking I'm off the notion.'

' Would you not like one of the New Houses ? '

' You mean—the Corporation kind ? '

' Uhhuh. They say they're awful easy kept clean.'

' So I suppose, but they're awful difficult to get. You've to
wait for months.'

In an attempt to be helpful, Mrs. McLeather asked if Sarah
knew anybody who ' worked in the Corporation.' On being
told that she didn't, Mrs. McLeather said, ' Well, it's funny, but
my neighbour was telling me just this morning that she's very
friendly with a woman whose sister's got a girl that's just started
going-set with a chap that works in the Gas Office. If you like,
I'll speak to my neighbour and see if she can do anything for
you.'

Sarah hesitated, not so much from reluctance to engage the
services of such an out-of-the-way connection, as from timidity
and the recollection of her husband's thrawnness.

' You should do what I do,' said Mrs. McLeather, noting the
hesitation. ' Greet for something miles beyond what you really
want, and then your man thinks he's no end of a hero when he
makes you climb down to what you wanted at the start.'

' That's an idea ! ' agreed Sarah. ' I know what I'll do ! I'll
let-on I'm determined to get a bought house—you know, one of
these semi-detached villas Mrs. M'Cotton was talking about
the other night—or a bungalow. All the same, I don't
suppose it would do any harm just to mention it to your
neighbour.'

An hour later Mrs. McLeather rushed home to attend to her
husband's dinner, and their conversation had been so engrossing
that it wasn't until she was half-way home that she remembered

the reason for her call, namely to get the address of the woman from whom the McFlannels had rented a coast house the previous year.

As a tactician, Sarah decided not to mention the matter of their removal to her husband during his dinner-hour. She had removed all traces of her spring-cleaning activities, and, instead of the sliced sausage-meat she had intended for his midday meal, she scurried down to the butcher's and got a succulent piece of Pope's Eye steak. It was just too bad that, owing to her excitement, it wasn't as well cooked as it might have been, and it turned out so tough that Lassie had to be given what baffled Willie's molars. About eight o'clock at night she ordered Maisie and Peter off to bed, Matt and Polly both being out on ploys of their own. Seven-year-old Peter felt it was an insult to be sent to bed at that hour, and said so. As for Maisie, she pleaded for ' just five minutes more.'

' No, you can't get five minutes more ! ' snapped her mother, whose apprehensions were making her irritable. ' No, it's no use looking at your father. You should know by this time that he's dead to the world when he's reading the paper.'

She regretted her sarcasm immediately it was uttered, but Willie was oblivious, even as she had said, and the door had been closed on the two children for fully two minutes before Sarah heaved a melodramatic sigh and began her attack.

' My ! What a day this has been ! '

' Mmmm ? ' grunted Willie nonchalantly.

' I did the kitchen shelves this morning, and what a time I had of it—climbing up and down the steps answering the door. First it was sticks, then it was a girl canvassing for vacuum cleaners, then——'

Willie turned a page of his newspaper. ' Ach,' he said, ' cheer up. Ye never died a winter yet.'

Ugh—so that was the kind of mood he was in !

After a moment or two Willie said, ' Then ? '

' Oh, never mind ! ' Her voice was sharp with nervousness. ' Just you read your paper ! Maybe you haven't read the advertisements yet ! '

Oblivious to the sarcasm and as though anxious to please her, he answered, ' Neither Ah have ! Here's an advert. for an unction sale. How would you like : " A grand piano. Lady going abroad. With carved legs." He sniggered at the juxtaposition of the words, but was unprepared for the defiance of Sarah's retort that she would like it fine.

' Oh-ho !' exclaimed Willie, putting down the paper at last. ' So that's the wey o't ! Ah jist thoght when Ah came in the night that there wis a kinna ambeetious look in yer eye. Whit is't this time ? A new hat ? '

' No.'

' Then it's a vacuum cleaner. That lassie that wis at the door——'

' No, it's not ! At least——'

' Ah see. Well, come on an' sit doon an' tell us a' aboot it. The sooner you let me know whit it is ye want, the sooner Ah'll let ye know ye're no' gettin' it. See ? '

Sarah stopped fiddling with the stocking she was pretending to darn. Now for it ! She gulped. ' It—it's a new house.'

Willie looked uncomfortable, almost startled. Or was that just his birse getting up ? ' How ? ' he demanded. ' Whit's up wi' this yin ? '

' Oh, everything ! It's so dirty for one thing. And there's no decent place for drying the clothes, and——'

' My, but you're the one for changin' yer mind !' said Willie derisively. ' When we flitted in here five year ago it had a' the virtues o' paradise. The top flat was gonnae be that clean, an' it wis gonnae be that handy fur me at ma work, an'——'

' That's all very well, but if we can get a better place, why should we go on staying here—where there's no place for Maisie and Peter to play but round about the ashpits.'

' Ach, don't let that worry ye ! It never did me ony hairm when Ah wis a boy.'

Sarah tried another line. ' But, Willie, now that you're a foreman don't you think it's only right that we should clear out of this cheap house and leave it for somebody that can't afford anything better ? '

'Here, Serah!' exclaimed Willie in mock alarm, 'you've been readin' *The Daily Bugle*!'

'Aw, don't make a fool of me, Willie,' she pleaded—a wistful note creeping into her voice. 'I was just thinking to-day how nice it would be to have a house of our very own—a bungalow, say, with our own bit of ground round about it. We could easy put down fifty pounds——'

'Here!' This time the alarm in Willie's voice was genuine. 'Easy on, there! Ye're no' suggestin' we should *buy* a hoose, are ye?'

'Of course!' Sarah told herself to keep calm. 'Why not?'

'Jist because Ah'm no' daft! The very idea! Workin'-class people like us buyin' a hoose!'

He really looked terribly angry, Sarah thought, but nevertheless she heaved another patient sigh and said, 'My, Willie, you're awful unreasonable! Just because you can't abide changes you think everybody else should be the same. D'you mind the time I wanted a carpet for the parlour? You were fair wild at me for suggesting such a thing—you said it was just me wanting to be up-sides with my neighbours, and now——'

'Well, so it was! An' very likely this notion ye've got o' buyin' a hoose is because Mrs. McTweed doon the stair has bought yin.'

'Oh, don't talk to me about that woman!' retorted Sarah vehemently, and then she wondered if perhaps she had given the show away by being too obvious. Willie, however, didn't seem to have noticed her aversion to her neighbour, for he continued:

'Naw, Serah, ye're doon the wrang lum this time. An' it's no' jist a bought hoose Ah'm up against—it's the very idea o' me diggin' a gairden. *Me!* Ah don't even know wan end o' a spade f'ae the ither—an' whit's mair, *Ah don't want tae know!*'

'But, Willie, think what we'd save—we could have home-grown vegetables and flowers, and after so-many years we'd have no rent to pay.'

'See here, Serah. Have you any idea hoo much it wid cost us tae take on a bought house? We'd need new furnicher.'

'No, we wouldn't!'

'Ay, but we would! Thae bungalows is that jerry-built they would drap doon deid if they saw yer mother's kist o' drawers ye're so prood o'.'

Wasn't he tantalizing! 'Is that meant for a joke?' she asked coldly.

'An' forbye there would be gairden tools an' seeds tae buy.'

'But we could make the most of the garden into grass!'

'Don't you bullieve it! You wid *hiv* tae be up-sides wi' yer neeburs.'

At the word 'neeburs' all the bitterness of Sarah's soul welled up. 'No, we wouldn't!' she declared. 'It's only in a tenement where your neighbours criticize you!' A whining note crept into her speech as she added, 'My, you're awful sticking! After me picturing to myself what it would be like to have nobody's dirt to clean but our own, and space for the children to play, and nice neighbours——'

'But, Serah, Ah'm tellin' ye—we cannae afford tae buy a hoose. Get that intae yer noddle. Ehm—unless . . .' and a crafty look came into Willie's eyes.

'Unless what?' The look had not escaped the searching gaze of his wife.

'Unless ye like tae ask ma auld auntie tae come and stey wi' us.'

What was he up to now, wondered Sarah. Old Auntie was the skeleton which is to be found in most family cupboards, and Sarah tried to ignore the situation by pointing out that the dirty old woman wasn't her relation and that she wouldn't have her in her house at any price.

'They say she's got a gey pickle siller, an' she'd pey 'er way.'

'Don't suggest such a thing!' cried Sarah, on the verge of tears. 'That woman's a disgrace to the family!'

'Well, then, ye'll jist need tae get rid o' yer high-falutin' notions. If Mrs. McTweed's makin' the place too hot fur ye——'

'I never said a word about Mrs. McTweed!'

'Maybe no' the nicht, but Ah've had that wumman tae ma

tea every blessed nicht fur years, an' Ah'm fed up hearin' aboot 'er.' A change came over Willie's voice. 'Whit you should look fur is a nice hoose, one stair up, wi' wooden banisters an' a stained-gless staircase windy. Ye'd jist be in yer element in a place like that.'

Was there ever such a man! Sarah, like Mrs. McTweed, looked upwards towards the ceiling. The sight of the pulleys and what was hanging on them brought her thoughts back to earth again. 'But I'm tired of living in a tenement!'

Willie folded his arms and looked thrawn. Was it possible that he was fighting a battle of his own? 'Well,' he said at length. 'Ye heard whit Ah said aboot a gairden!'

'But, Willie, I'm quite willing to look after a garden. And if it was too much for me, Polly or Matt would give me a hand. You would never need to touch it!'

The man seemed oddly eager. 'Is that a bargain?'

'It is—it is!' exclaimed Sarah with equal alacrity.

'Do you promise me on yer word of honour that ye'll never as much as ask me tae tickle a plant?'

Oh dear-dear! Things looked excitingly hopeful! The words came tumbling out of Sarah's trembling mouth, 'I'll promise you anything if you'll only take me out of here!'

'Would ye be willin' tae go intae a Corporation hoose?'

'But, Willie, think of the advantages of a bought house!' It would never do to surrender too quickly.

'Bocht hoose yer granny! Ah'm askin' ye tae meet me hauf-wey.'

'Well—oh—all right.'

'An' will ye stick tae yer promise aboot the gairden?'

'I will that! You'll never need to touch it!'

'Well, then, ya silly wee chookie, whit-fur could ye no' have said that at the very beginnin'?' He fumbled in his pocket. 'Here's me been sittin' wi' somethin' that's been burnin' a hole in ma pooch a' night. It's a caird Ah got off the postie this mornin'—it's f'ae the Corporation aboot a hoose Ah put in fur six months ago. Read it.'

Ignoring the outstretched hand with its contents, Sarah flung an arm round her husband's neck. ' Aw, Willie, fancy you thinking about that. That was awful decent of you. You're just the nicest——'

Willie struggled for air, a triumphant gleam appearing on his face as he exclaimed, ' Heh, haud off, haud off ! Ye're spilin' ma shed ! ' But Sarah, her face buried in her husband's shoulder, missed the triumphant gleam ; already her thoughts were busy with calculations about curtains and linoleum and carpets.

CHAPTER 7

UP IN THE WORLD

THE sound of Polly's key in the door wakened Sarah from her happy dreams in her husband's arms. She rushed to meet the girl, crying, ' Polly ! You'll never guess ! We've got a new house ! '

Polly, who had been looking forward to creating a sensation on her own account, felt rather deflated, but her mother's news was startling enough to cause her to say, in the genteel way she had adopted within the last week or two, ' Oh, goody-goody ! Where ? '

' Knightswood ! ' Sarah consulted the card again. ' Twenty-three Gartnavel Crescent—four apartments ! '

' Four apartments ! ' echoed the girl. ' Can I have a room to myself ? '

' Ay. The scullery ! ' put in her father, who was peeved that she wasn't curious as to how they had obtained the house.

Sarah, however, was indignant. ' Well, I like that ! ' she exclaimed. ' What's to happen to the rest of the family if you get a room to yourself ? '

' 's'easy ! ' replied Polly. ' There'll be a living-room and three bedrooms.'

' Two bedrooms ! ' corrected Sarah. ' One living-room, one sitting-room, and *two* bedrooms ! '

' Three bedrooms and *no* sitting-room ! ' insisted Polly.

' No sitting-room ? ' Sarah wondered what heresy this was.

' No ! ' retorted the girl, who, by virtue of her employment as a Sheriff Officer's junior typist and message girl, felt qualified to speak with authority on matters pertaining to property. ' No sitting-room ! '

' I never heard such blethers ! ' Sarah turned to Willie who was fondling the dog on his knee. ' D'you hear her ? ' she demanded.

'Ay,' said Willie, 'it's a black look-oot fur the country if folks isnae tae get sittin'-room mantelpieces fur their black marble clocks!'

'Mother!' exclaimed Polly. 'Surely you won't take that old-fashioned thing with you to the new house.'

Sarah ignored the plea; the subject was wandering from its objective. 'Never you mind the clock!' she ordered. 'What d'you mean—saying there's no sitting-room?'

'Just what I say—*no* sitting-room! The Corporation says that folk have always been in the habit of sitting in their kitchen —just like us—so they make a big living-room with a coal fireplace.'

'Does that mean there's no fireplaces in the other rooms?' gulped Sarah.

'Sometimes. So—seeing there's three bedrooms, can I have one to myself? You and Dad'll be sleeping in the living-room, won't you?'

'Ay here, Serah,' said Willie, jerking his thumb over his shoulder. 'Whit aboot this feather-bed here?'

'Oh, I thought we'd get one of those new divan beds—you know, the kind you can fold up the blankets and pillows and everything inside.'

'Ay, Ah know!' said Willie. 'There wis a chap in the work came in one day hirplin' like a chair that's lost its hind legs. "Whit's up wi' ye?" says Ah. "Ach," says he, "Ah fell comin' oota bed this mornin'. Thae new divan beds has that much steelwork in them the Forth Bridge isnae in it!"' To which remark Sarah gave such a contemptuous snort that her husband found it difficult to reconcile her attitude with that of the woman who had been so tender half an hour earlier.

'Look here,' said Polly, 'you'll have a great big scullery— kitchenette, it's called. This kitchen furniture can go into it. The parlour suite can go into the living-room.'

'And get all tashed in a fortnight?' demanded Sarah.

Willie put Lassie down, spanked her playfully, and sent her off to her basket at the warmer side of the grate, saying, 'Ach, Serah, thae auld bits o' sticks isnae owin' ye anythin'!'

71

'Then buy a new suite, Mother!' suggested Polly with enthusiasm.

'You hold your tongue!' answered Sarah sharply. 'We'll have enough to spend our money on if we've to buy a divan bed—and other things forbye.' She looked at the linoleum at her feet. 'This stuff'll never see another floor.'

'You'll need to buy a proper dining-table,' Polly pointed out. 'But if you took the mirror-back off the sideboard, what's left would look fairly modern.'

This suggestion so offended Sarah that it was quite a little while before she was calm enough to go on with the discussion. And then Polly had to spoil the party all over again by saying, 'What are you going to do with the atrocities?'

When Sarah had had it explained to her that Polly was referring to the pair of pictures which flanked the overmantel in the parlour, she was furious. 'You impiddent bizzum!' she exclaimed. 'These pictures were painted by your Uncle Peter when he was a car conductor!'

'Huh!' sneered Polly. 'One hand with the paint-brush and the other punching tickets.'

Willie sniggered. He had always been suspicious of the artistic quality of his brother-in-law's handiwork, but he had been so impressed by the grandeur of the gilt frames, and so overwhelmingly reminded of the pictures' magnificence as a marriage present during all his married life that he had hitherto held his peace. Sarah, on the other hand, was very huffed. She got up and made the supper in vindictive silence. Just as they were sitting down at the table, Matt came in looking rather unhappy. At fifteen he was an odd boy, fond still of reading what his mother called trash, but no longer interested in football. The spectacles he had taken to wearing did not improve his appearance. He had that day been reminded he had not yet returned his School Report with his father's signature on it. All evening he had been walking the streets worrying about what excuse he would offer to his parents for the facts contained in the Report. It wasn't his father he minded so much—it was his mother. She was so anxious for him to be clever, to be dux of the class—of the school. She had even told everybody he was coming-out-for a teacher.

The boy squatted on the floor beside Lassie's basket. That was one thing about a dog—it liked you whether you were clever or not. That old School Report would have to be signed to-night. Was there no chance of getting Dad alone? Sarah called him sharply to the table. Getting up, he joined the others and sat unmoved while they all began to tell him about the new house. After a bit Polly said :

'If I get a room of my own, Mother, I'll keep it clean myself.'

'Don't you say another word about a room of your own !' snapped Sarah. 'If Matt is coming-out-for a teacher, it's him that'll need to get a room to himself, so's he can study in peace and quiet. Isn't that right, son ? '

Matt looked and felt miserable. Teacher ! When all he wanted from life was to leave school and go to work somewhere —anywhere. Polly saw the misery on his face and, with the cruelty of adolescence, gloated over it.

'Coming-out-for a teacher !' she taunted. 'Some hope ! Matt's nothing but a round O.'

A moment later she regretted what she had said, not because she was sorry for hurting Matt's feelings, but because she saw from the antagonism on her mother's face that she had jeopardized her own scheme for a room to herself in the new house.

'Don't you *dare* speak like that about your brother !' shouted Sarah. As she spoke she reached out a protecting hand towards Matt, who cringed away from the caress. Willie sat by silently. This partiality of Sarah's for Matt had often disturbed him, but feeling he could only do harm by mentioning the matter he had always held his peace. In any case he had a shrewd suspicion that he himself wasn't entirely guiltless, for wee Maisie had always meant a good deal more to him than any of the others. All the same he had better say something. He cleared his throat. 'Come on, Matt ! Can ye no' gie Polly tit-for-tat ? '

Matt shook his head. 'She's quite right,' he mumbled.

'She is not !' exclaimed his mother, 'and the sooner she apologizes the better it'll be for her.'

But Polly was quite unrepentant and said so with her shoulders and her eyebrows.

' Hae ye nae spunk in ye, Matt ? ' asked Willie.

' Oh, leave me alone ! ' The boy shrugged his mother's hand from his neck. This wasn't making things any easier for the signing of the Report. The general atmosphere of discomfort increased. Sarah was broadcasting waves of indignation ; Matt's contribution was misery ; Willie's was concerned with conflicting loyalties, while Polly's was sheer defiance. Nobody spoke. Suddenly there was a wheenge from the basket at the side of the grate. They all turned round, and there was Lassie—sitting up on her rear, her front paws tucked in in an agony of anxiety.

' Aw,' exclaimed Willie who was the first to divine the dog's attitude, ' the wee sowl's askin' us tae stop quarrellin'. Come here, pet ! '

But the dog was concentrating on Polly. Her eyes seemed big with distress. ' Speak tae the wee thing, Polly,' urged Willie.

The girl got down on her knees beside the swaying little figure. ' What is it, Lassie ? ' she asked gently. Immediately the dog's tongue flashed out and licked Polly's face. ' You're a wee dodger, so you are ! ' she went on, all the venom gone from her voice. Lifting the dog she went back to the table, and, stroking the shaggy coat to hide her embarrassment, she said, ' Sorry, Matt. I—I didn't mean to—to hurt you.'

Matt nodded his head indifferently. He knew he wasn't smart, but at least he had the wit to recognize the limitation of her apology. Oh well, what did it matter ? For a few minutes the family fussed over Lassie, tossing bits of food to her ; then Willie, proud of the latest trick he had taught her, let her sniff a piece of cheese. Walking over to the door with the cheese, he opened it a few inches and placed the morsel on the top of the door. When he had counted three Lassie bounded to the door, slammed it shut with the force of her leap on it, and was on to the dropping cheese before it had reached the ground. Everybody was delighted with the performance. It deserved an encore —and got it.

The slamming of the door wakened Peter, who stole in in his pyjamas complaining of hunger, and by the time he had been fed and told about the new house, peace had been restored completely. Sarah accompanied him back to the parlour where she tucked him in beneath the blankets, while Polly seized the opportunity to slip to the bedroom, where she tiptoed around for fear of wakening Maisie and having to tell her a story before the child would go to sleep again. The door opened.

' Here,' said Sarah, with a faint echo of her earlier asperity, ' where were you to-night ? '

' At the pictures ! '

' Who with ? Mary McMuslin ? '

' No. I was out with a boy ! '

' What ! ' exclaimed Sarah in a hoarse whisper. ' You never told me ! What boy is this ? Not Dick M'Cotton, I hope ! '

' No fear ! It's a boy that works in the County Buildings ! ' The girl tried to make it sound casual, but succeeded only in making herself look foolish.

' Works in the County Buildings ! ' Sarah was deeply impressed. ' You mean—he's a lawyer ? '

' No, he's something to do with the Summary Court.' Actually the duties of the youth in question were confined mostly to posting letters and keeping the Sheriff Clerk's fire stoked, but with an ambitious mother like Sarah, Polly couldn't resist the temptation to exaggerate. She was rewarded by seeing her mother enraptured.

' What's his name ? '

' McPlush. Donald McPlush.'

' Where does he stay ? '

' Mosspark.'

Sarah's satisfaction found expression in the rising inflection of her ' Imphm ! ' She added : ' Did he see you home ? '

' No fear ! You surely don't think I'd let him know I lived in this dump ! '

Sarah understood—and sympathized. ' Are you seeing him again ? '

' Of course ! ' said Polly. After all, the fellow *did* say :

75

' Cheerio—see you at the counter to-morrow ' when he left her at the corner of Crow Road.

Meanwhile Matt, in the kitchen, was unearthing his School Report from his case. Was there any chance that his father would be so excited about this new house that he would sign it without scrutiny ?

' What's this ? ' asked Willie.

' My School Report. Will you sign it, please ? '

Willie peered at it. ' Mathematics—45. Is that out of 50 ? '

He was for it ! Matt gulped. ' No. A hundred.'

' Mn ? Science 51. English 97—that's a guid mark, son ! French 47. Latin 44.'

' Please, Dad ! ' whispered Matt hoarsely. ' Sign it ! Quick ! Before Mother comes back ! '

' Ah'm afraid ye havenae been stickin' in at yer lessons,' countered Willie unmoved by the pleading.

Matt, for his part, ignored the remark, placing instead a pen, ink, and blotting-paper in front of his father. Oh, if he would only sign it quick !

' Ah'm thinkin' yer mother'll be gey disappointed wi' this, Matt ! '

' Uhha ! '

' D'ye no' like the school ? '

' I hate it ! ' The intensity of the boy's expression amazed his father.

' How can ye come out for a teacher if ye hate the school ? '

' I don't want to be a teacher ! It's Mother that's—that's got a bee in her bonnet ! '

' Eh-eh ! ' warned Willie. ' That's no' the wey tae talk aboot yer mother.'

' I don't care ! ' (Why couldn't he get on with the signing ?) ' I don't want to be a teacher ! '

' Whit else wid ye like tae be ? '

' I don't know. Anything ! Oh, Dad—here's Mother ! Sign it ! Quick ! '

Willie put a hasty ' W. McFlannel ' on the dotted line, re-flecting with pride that the lad had a decent streak in him or he surely would have imitated the childish signature himself. There was, too, a certain satisfaction in being confided in by Sarah's favourite. But Sarah had turned into the bedroom. They were safe for a few more minutes.

'Wid ye like tae be an engineer, son?'

Matt shook his head.

'Well, whit aboot bein' a joiner or a carpenter—makin' furniture. Eh?'

The head was still shaking, so, patiently, Willie continued: 'A painter, then? Or what aboot learnin' tae be an engine-driver? Ye were aye efter bein' an engine-driver when ye were wee.'

But Matt's tastes had evidently changed, for the negative motion of his head was more emphatic than ever.

'Is there nothin' ye like daein', son?'

'Yes—reading books, and writing composition and essays and grammar.'

Willie sighed. What could a 'common five-eighth' of a father do with a son like this? He tried again, going through a long list of trades, none of which included the obvious one. Sarah's return to the kitchen broke up the interview, and Matt went off to bed with the signed Report safely hidden in the copy of *Kidnapped*, which he had been carrying about with him for days under the oxter of his jersey. Willie determined to open his campaign on Matt's behalf right away. He cleared his throat:

'Ehm—Serah—Ah wis jist thinkin'—aboot Matt—d'ye no' think it's no' fair tae shove him on at school if he's no' wantin' tae be a teacher?'

'How? What's worrying you? The money?'

Willie scowled at the injustice of the retort, but he merely said: 'Naw—Ah wis worryin' aboot the boy hissel'.'

'Well, you can stop worrying. I've made up my mind he's going to be a teacher, and none of his molliegruntin—or yours either—'ll make me change it.'

'And whit if he disnae pass 'is exams?'

Sarah sighed. Men were the limit. As sure as you wanted to keep in with them, to butter them up so's to put them in a

77

good tid for buying a whole lot of new furniture, they went and tried to pick a quarrel with you about something that didn't matter a docken. She decided to tackle the matter boldly.

'Never mind Matt just now!' she said. 'I want to talk to you about the new house. We'll need to buy a new bedroom suite for the boys' room.'

'Ay? And anither yin fur Polly's room?'

'Well—I was just thinking—right enough she's growing up —she's quite the young lady now. . . .'

Willie laughed. 'Whit's up yer sleeve noo, Serah?'

'Nothing. Only—she was telling me that she's been out with a boy to-night.'

'D'ye tell me that! Jings, Serah, we must be gettin' auld!'

'That's right. And he works in the County Buildings— coming-out-for a Sheriff.' Sarah got the exaggeration out without the slightest quiver of conscience.

'Ye're a great wee lass, Serah. But here—sit doon. Ah've been daein' a bit o' thinkin' masel'.' He turned round to make sure the door was shut, then continued in a hoarse whisper: 'We've got over three hundred in the Bank. Whit d'ye say tae spendin' two hundred on the new hoose—fur furniture an' things. A new pianna. It's time Maisie wis gettin' a better instrument tae learn on.'

Sarah gaped. This was her wildest dream come true—but she didn't want it like that. She wanted to fight for it tooth-and-nail, to feel the triumph of winning it from a stingy husband who grudged her everything. She wasn't sure now that she wanted anything at all. She argued against the expenditure for a quarter of an hour and then gave in gracefully. After that the pair of them sat by the fireside until midnight discussing new furnishings with all the eagerness of a recently engaged couple.

The result was that the second flitting of their married lives was conducted with a good deal less fuss and indignity than the first, Sarah taking great pride in the fact that the new furniture was delivered to the new house not in a plain van, but in one that proclaimed in large gilt letters that its owners dealt for cash only. Polly got her own way in the matter of the bedroom, but not with regard to Uncle Peter's pictures, for they still flanked the overmantel of the living-room fireplace on which stood the marble clock and the rearing horsemen, all of them anachronisms that the girl bitterly resented. Everybody was happy, except Maisie who was too young to appreciate the luxury of solitude at night, and except Matt who hated having to look after a garden, and except Peter who missed his old chums and the washing-houses for playgrounds, and except Polly who was afraid the young gentleman in the County Buildings was cooling off after hearing that she lived in such a common place as Knightswood, and except Willie who was depressed by the fact that, living so far away from his work, he couldn't get home for a midday meal. Sarah, however, more than made up for the others in happiness. Often she would stop in the middle of her washing to take an admiring look at the bedrooms with their white paint and new curtains and carpets and down quilts, as well as the interior grate in the living-room that needed no blackleading, to say nothing of the new piano. Black it was. Plain black—no candlesticks or fretwork, with a good strong tone. My, my ! What would her mother think if she could see her now ! The McFlannels were real swells—eating their meals off a dining-table (polished oak with pull-out leaves) and sitting, not on hard kitchen chairs, but on (near) leather-covered ones. Admittedly the chairs gave you a stab between the shoulders if you leant back, but they looked real handsome. She must ask Mrs. McTweed up some afternoon. And Mrs. McLeather—on a different day, of course. Oh, and Mrs. M'Cotton. My, wouldn't Mrs. M'Cotton be chawed when she saw how grand everything was ! In spite of all her boastings about bungalows and semi-detached villas, the M'Cottons were still living in the same old two-room-and-kitchen in Partick Road—and here was the McFlannel family in a four-apartment house ! Yes, she would run down the very next day and invite the M'Cottons up for tea.

That night Willie came home from his work, and, after complaining about how long it took him to get home nowadays, he added : ' Ah came up the road wi' Jim M'Cotton the now.'

' Did you ? What was he doing in this district ? '

' He wis on 'is wey up tae see their new hoose. It's in the next street. A five-apartment.'

' A five-apartment ! ' shrieked Sarah. ' But they've only two of a family—Dick and wee Jean ! '

Willie proceeded stolidy with his ablutions in the scullery. That was one thing about Sarah—you could always depend on her carrying on in the same old way every time she got news she didn't like. You got used to it, even when, as now, she went on hour after hour. ' Just two of a family ! It's a crying shame, so it is ! There's been some jookery-packery going on somewhere ! A five-apartment house ! '

Was it her imagination or had some of the furniture really lost its glory, Sarah wondered.

CHAPTER 8

MATT—THE MISFIT

A YEAR or two flashed by and it was tea-time. Sarah, bustling and breathless, sat down beside the cosy and the new half tea-set. Everything looked real nice, she thought. Six people could sit round a table so tidily—Willie up there at the other end (she would be better not to look at him too affectionately or he would be wondering what she was wanting money for next) ; Matt and Peter on one side, Polly and Maisie on the other, with Lassie at ' hopeful corner ' between Willie and Matt. She would never admit it to Polly, but the new oval mirror above the fireplace did look very much better than the old-fashioned overmantel, and the mahogany clock with the Westminster chimes didn't remind her of a graveyard the way the old marble one had done after Polly had put the idea into her head. Polly was getting to be a nippy one. She was still working at that Sheriff Officer's place—a senior typist now, although she seemed to miss going the messages to the Court. What had come between her and that McPlush boy from Mosspark ? Children nowadays never seemed to con- fide in their mothers. Just look at Matt. He was in the third year at the Higher Grade for the second session ! Somehow he seemed to be awful sulky these days—didn't know what was good for him. Silly notions, he had, about not wanting to be a teacher —didn't realize how thankful he'd be yet for his mother pushing him. Peter was going to be nippy, like Polly. Always had an answer ready for you. He'd make a better teacher than Matt— but there, you mustn't think thoughts like that. Matt's teachers don't understand him, that's all. And anyway, he reads far too many trashy books. Maisie doesn't seem to be growing out of her girniness. There she is—at it again. Sarah opened her mouth to speak, but Willie got in first with :

' Whit's up wi' ye, Maisie ? Sittin' there wi' a face like a torn melodeon ! '

' I don't like marconi cheese ! '

81

'Mac-ar-oni cheese!' corrected Polly.

'Well—mac-ar-oni cheese!' repeated Maisie. 'I don't like it!'

'Neither do I,' said Peter.

'Nobody likes it except Matt,' observed Polly, 'but he's his mother's pet!'

Sarah was angry. 'There's no such thing in this house as a mother's pet!' she blazed. 'You know perfectly well that it's impossible to please the lot of you. We had scrambled eggs last night, Polly, because you like it.'

'But,' countered Polly, 'we had macaroni cheese three nights ago!'

Meanwhile Maisie was sitting well back in her chair determination and disgust registered on her face. 'Ach, come on,' urged her father. 'Ah'll try ye a race. See who's done first.'

'I don't want to try a race!' sulked Maisie.

'You're a wee footer!' declared Sarah. 'There never was a family like this for grumbling about their food. And when I ask you what I'll make for a change, you all say: "Oh make anything you like."'

'Ach, cheer up . . .' began Willie, when the family took up the chorus and finished it along with him: 'ye never died a winter yet!'

'That's right,' said Willie good-humouredly, 'make a fool o' yer auld faither.'

But the chorus still seemed to be echoing in Sarah's ears; in any case it had to be pretty loud to overcome the torrent of music that was coming from the wireless set.

'Don't shout like that!' she ordered. 'The neighbours will hear you. I used to think Mrs. McTweed was bad, but the ones round here are ten times worse.'

For a moment or two no-one spoke and the wireless set had it all its own way. Maisie ate her 'kitchen' in such a slovenly manner that most of it found its way to the floor and thence to Lassie's mouth. Lassie was a nice wee dog—Maisie patted the dark grey head surreptitiously.

'I say!' exclaimed Polly suddenly. 'That's awful bilge

that's on the wireless just now. See if we can't get a dance band,' and she rose to adjust the wavelength.

'Ye'll jist leave it !' ordered her father. 'There's nothin' tae bate a Sousa March,' and he strummed on the table with his knife and fork in rhythm with the music.

Polly reseated herself and initiated a discussion about broadcast entertainment, which showed that no two of the family shared the same tastes ; it lasted for a lively five minutes, until Maisie pointed out that Peter had had three white crusts, one after the other. This Peter denied, and thereafter the two youngest carried on an argument that lasted till Maisie took refuge in tears and Sarah had to interfere.

'Be quiet !' shouted Sarah above the din of verbal battle. 'Every one of you ! The neighbours'll be complaining.'

Once again the only sound that could be heard was the wireless set.

'Here,' snapped Polly, 'that band's getting on my nerves. Can't we get anything else ? Mother—pass over the *Radio Times*, please !'

'I'll do nothing of the kind !' answered Sarah. 'I'm just as able to read as you !' She reached behind her for the journal, thumbed its pages, and then announced, 'It's a Gaylic Concert.'

The fruitiness of Willie's 'Ach !' conveyed the impression that he was not an advocate of the cause of the bi-lingual Gael ; Matt, however, contributed the observation that, according to his English teacher, the word should be pronounced ' Gahlic.'

'How does *he* know,' demanded Sarah, 'if he's an Englishman ?'

'Ah—ya silly poultice !' sneered Matt, 'I never——'

There was a shuffling of chair legs as Willie instantaneously reached across, and, giving Matt a cuff on the jaw, said, 'Take that—fur talkin' tae yer mother as if she wis one o' yer school pals !'

Matt, surprised and injured, both mentally and physically, fondled his jaw. 'That was sore !' he complained.

'It'll be sorer in a minute if ye don't apologize !' stormed his father.

Sarah tried to smooth matters over, saying, ' Ugh, never mind.'

Willie, however, looked so threatening that Maisie began to whimper. ' Ay, but Ah will mind ! ' he yelled. ' Come on, Matt. Apologize ! '

On the borders of sixteen, though, it isn't so easy to be diplomatic. ' I will not ! ' exclaimed Matt. ' It was a daft thing to say. Everybody knows that an English teacher is a teacher of English.'

' Ay,' commented Willie grimly, ' everybody but the auld fools that's peyin' fur your eddication. Are ye gonnae apologize, or . . .'

Matt got up, pushing his chair away with the backs of his legs. ' I'm going out ! ' he announced. ' On my bike ! '

' You are not ! ' said Sarah. ' You'll sit down again and finish your tea.'

But Matt was by now half-way to the door, saying, ' I won't ! '

' Ach, let'm go ! ' advised Willie. ' Maybe he'll take a tummle tae 'imsel'.'

' But Matt,' called Sarah as the door opened, ' you promised to weed the garden to-night ! '

' To pot with the garden ! '

Matt was closing the door after him, when Peter shouted, ' Aw, Matt, you said you'd help me with my geometry ! '

' Huh ! ' Matt peered round the edge of the door. ' Ask Mother to help you ! ' On the Parthian shot he shut the door, very loudly.

' Oh dear ! ' wailed Sarah, ' and the garden's in such a state with weeds that the neighbours'll be complaining.'

' Ach, forget aboot yer neeburs ! ' snapped Willie who was feeling embarrassed. ' D'ye no' mind afore we flittit here, yer one cry wis tae get oota the tenement so's ye could have nice neeburs. Says you, " It's only in a tenement where yer neighbours criticize you ! " '

At that Polly sniggered—a gesture that so riled her mother that she poked the girl roughly on the arm, saying, ' What's the giggle for ? '

' I'm tickled to death at the fact that the only one who likes macaroni cheese has gone away and left it.'

' I don't want any more,' declared Maisie, putting her plate on the floor defiantly.

' Neither do I,' said Peter, and in a moment Lassie was running from one plate to the other in an agony of indecision as to which was the bigger plateful.

With the family now in open revolt, Sarah was in a dilemma. ' What am I to do ? ' she wailed. ' If we'd been nearer the shops we might've got hot pies.'

' Och, don't worry yersel',' said Willie, adding yet another plate to the cluster on the floor. ' This is the Edinburgh holiday —there'll no' be a hot pie left in Glasgow. See's ower the jam dish, Maisie ! '

For a few moments the strains of ' Blaze Away ' blazed away uninterrupted, until Peter said, ' I wish Matt hadn't gone out. I can't do my geometry myself.'

' Maybe Ah'll can gi'e ye a haun' wi't, son,' said Willie with paternal omniscience. ' Wait tae the tea's cleared away, we'll get the table.'

To this arrangement Polly objected, though, on the grounds that she wanted to cut out a frock for herself and, while she and her mother were arguing about the vulnerability of a polished oak surface, Peter kept up a drumming accompaniment to the wireless music by thumping on the legs of his chair with his heels.

' Stop that ! ' His mother turned on him suddenly. ' And, Willie—she reached out to the wireless set—' I think I'll put down the volume a bit.'

' Naw don't ! If ye put it doon ony faurer we'll no' hear wur ain set fur the yin through the wall ! '

' Well, I'll put it off altogether ! '

' Then we'll hear hauf a dizzen sets at the same time ! '

' But my head's *deaved* ! ' Sarah's sense of injury brought her voice to a shriek.

' Oh, all right ! Anything fur a quiet wife ! ' The music stopped abruptly, with a plop of contempt ; the silence was bliss. As the table was being cleared, Willie turned to Peter and said,

'Well, son, come on ower tae the fire an' let me see whit's worryin' ye aboot yer g'ography.'

'It's not g'ography—it's g'ometry!' replied Peter impatiently. He scrabbled among the books in his school-case and brought out a third-hand volume. 'It's a new theorem we got to-day, and I can't understand it.'

Willie took the book, peered at the open page, and said, 'Whit's this?—"In a right-angled triangle the square on the hip-hip——"' He stopped short without uttering the 'hooray' that rose to his lips.

'*Hy*-potenuse,' said Peter, returning Polly's wink.

'*Hy*-potenuse? They didnae hae thae kinna beasts at the school Ah wis at! Ah don't know whit things is comin' tae! When Ah wis your age——'

'Oh, don't tell us again, Dad!' pleaded Polly.

'I think I'll just go out and play for a wee while,' said Peter. 'Matt'll tell me when he comes home.'

Sarah, *en route* for the kitchenette, stopped, saying, 'You'll go out and play none! You'll just do the rest of your lessons first. We don't send you to a Higher Grade School to waste your time playing!'

'Oh, Mother!' exclaimed Polly. 'Do try to remember there's no Higher Grades nowadays!'

'Whit's that ye say, Polly?' asked her father.

'I said—there's no Higher Grades nowadays.'

'Oh? Ah woulda thought an eddicated young lady like you woulda said "there *are* no Higher Grades nowadays"!'

Polly tossed her head and left the room; Sarah, to avoid showing how glad she felt at her elder daughter's discomfiture, turned on her younger one with:

'Come on, Maisie. It's time for you to start your practice. You'll never learn to play the piano if you don't do it every day. You know what your teacher said!'

But Maisie remained sulking on her chair at the table. 'I don't want to learn the piano!' she mumbled.

'Then you'll be the only girl in your class that can't play, and how would you like that?'

' I don't care ! '

' Well, *I* care ! So, come on ! '

' The teacher said the last time that—that I didn't have it in me ! '

' Well, I like that ! ' gulped Sarah. ' What does he think we're paying him twenty-five shillings a quarter for if it's not to *put* it into you ? You sit down at the piano there when you're told ! '

Maisie slithered in the general direction of the instrument of torture, while her father, realizing his scholastic limitations, shut Peter's book and returned it to him, saying :

' Ehm, Serah—if Maisie's gonnae be ticklin' the ivories, Ah think Ah'll away oot fur a bit dauner. Comin', Lassie ? ' The dog threw herself upon his legs in an ecstasy as Willie shoved a battered old hat on his head. He slapped his daughter deftly as she was about to sit down on the piano stool, saying, ' Stick in, Maisie, seein' ye cannae be guid-lookin' ye'll need tae try an' be clever.'

Maisie, as much offended by her father's playful prod as by his remarks, burst into tears. ' Oh, Mother ! ' she wailed. ' Daddy's tormenting me ! '

' You shouldn't say things like that to her, Willie ! ' said Sarah. ' Shshsh, pet. Never you mind. You can play a lot better than *he*'ll ever do.'

Slamming the door behind him, Willie went away as happily as the dog at his feet, while Maisie sniffily opened the piano, and, finding the note ' D ' with the help of a chalk mark on the woodwork, she ascended and descended a succession of keynotes which she indifferently imagined to be a major scale. Her thoughts far away, the child was still shuffling over the same notes when, two minutes later, Polly returned to the living-room.

' My sainted aunt ! ' exclaimed the older girl, ' are you still at the same tune ? You were playing that weeks ago ! '

On the verge of fresh tears, Maisie replied, ' It's not a tune—it's a scale. And anyway, it's not the same one ! '

' Sounds the same—only worse ! ' retorted Polly.

' Oh, shut up ! ' barked Peter from the region of the dining-table, where he was sprawled among a scatter of books. ' How can I do any swotting when you two are kicking up a shindy like a couple of ragwifes ? '

' Away you go into your bedroom and do your lessons there ! ' suggested his mother.

' But there's no table there ! '

' You can make-do with the dressing-table ! . . . Maisie— you get on with your practice ! '

The boy gathered up his books while the piano-playing was renewed ; he left the room with a caustic remark that was fortunately missed by the pianist.

' Don't bang the door ! ' called his mother—a second too late. When the echoes had died away, she turned to Polly with a gesture of annoyance. ' That woman down the stair'll be up at me to complain about that door. I never thought I'd live to see the day when I'd've had a good word to say for Mrs. McTweed, but she was a lady compared with the trash around here.'

But Polly, at eighteen, could hardly be expected to enter into her mother's woes. She turned on her sister again : ' Oh, for any favour, Maisie, try your other hand. It'll at least be a change.'

' Mother,' moaned Maisie, ' now Polly's tormenting me ! '

' Never you heed Polly ! You're doing fine ! ' said Sarah, adding, ' I wish I could play half as well.'

All the same the child took the hint and, using her left hand, she produced the same noises an octave lower ; it was a weird achievement, containing neither rhythm nor consistency and never by any accident or design resulting in a diatonic scale, but Sarah, whose ear for music was as vague as her younger daughter's, thought it wonderful, and said so. Polly, however, thought differently.

' Oh, I can't stand that racket ! ' she snapped. ' I'm going out. If I hurry I'll maybe catch up with Dad and Lassie,' and she made for the door.

' Don't slam . . .' began Sarah, but once again she was too late.

In a moment or two Maisie got to work with both hands.

As she played, she kept her eyes fixed on a piece of music in front of her entitled : ' Oh where, tell me where, is your Highland Laddie gone ? ' but there was not much similarity between the pattern and the performance, the child unconsciously carrying out the Scriptural injunction to conceal from the left hand the activities of the right. As she toiled through her task, she leaned heavily on both pedals with her feet, no-one having noticed that the piano stool was too high for her. Suddenly the door was flung open and Peter tumbled in.

' Listen ! ' he stormed, ' I can't get peace to swot in there either ! There's two wireless sets going like mad across the street. Maisie's banging away here on the piano. There's a woman yowling down the stair and there's a baby crying somewhere. I'm going out ! '

' Well, just for half an hour,' conceded his mother, ' or you'll have to get up early in the morning to do your lessons.'

' O.K. chief ! '

' None of your O.K. chief to me ! '

' O.K. baby ! '

' Don't bang the door ! ' When the pictures had come to rest again after Peter's treatment of the door, his mother sighed and complained that it was small wonder her hair was going grey.

Maisie slid off the piano stool a few minutes later, announcing that she had finished her practice.

' You've only been at it for ten minutes ! ' protested Sarah.

' I've been at it for *hours* ! '

' My, you're getting as argumentative as your father ! I said *ten minutes* ! Go over the whole thing again ! '

With a shrewdness that was ever increasing in her, Maisie observed that the woman down the stair would be complaining, but before Sarah had completed her retort, the doorbell was ringing.

' I'll go ! ' said Maisie.

' You're not usually so eager ! Just you stay where you are.'

' But you're always saying how tired you are of running down the stairs to the door ! '

' Oh, all right. You go.'

Gleefully the child ran down the few steps to the door, opened it, and, finding no-one there, she was about to take the chance of escaping outside when her eye caught a small piece of paper lying on the doormat. She picked it up and went back to the living-room. Together, mother and daughter deciphered the pencilled note. ' Mrs. McFlannel. The plaster is coming off of our ceiling with the way your door is always being banged. If it happens again we will report you to the lord provost. Mrs. McRubber.'

Sarah gaped from the note to her daughter. Maisie, in an agony of desire to be helpful, suggested she might be better to stop her music.

' Oh, very well then. But just imagine putting a note like that through the door instead of coming to speak to me ! She's fly—she knows fine I'd have something to say to her about the way she's always leaving the garden gate open for all the dogs in the district to run in and out. Wait you—I'll send her a note that'll make her sit up ! '

' Can I get out to play for a wee while, then ? '

' Oh, all right. Don't bang the door for goodness' sake.'

But alas, Maisie's eagerness to be gone was so great that the door was shut as vigorously as ever and Sarah began to wonder if, with a heedless family like hers, she could afford to take up the cudgels with Mrs. McRubber. She was still pondering the point when the outside door opened, footsteps came cautiously up the stairs and Matt came into the living-room.

' Oh, it's you, son ! ' exclaimed Sarah affectionately. ' Come in. Don't stand there ! There's nobody in but me, and I'm not going to eat you ! '

Matt stood where he was and blurted out shamefacedly that he was sorry.

' That's all right. It was stupid of me to say the thing. I've kept your macaroni cheese warm for you. Had you a nice run on your bike ? '

The boy, grateful for the casual way his mother was treating the affair, advanced a few steps into the room. ' I wasn't—out —on my bike,' he murmured.

' No ? Where were you ? '

'I—did—some weeding in the back garden. I didn't want the others to see me.'

A warm glow spread itself throughout his mother's being. He was a grand boy, was Matt. She felt she could have given him half her kingdom. All of it, in fact.

'Mother!' Matt had by now reached the fireside where he kicked the fender in an agony of courage and self-consciousness. 'Mother—I—please, won't you let me leave school? I—really—wouldn't make a good teacher. I hate the school so much!' It was out at last!

Sarah choked back her disappointment; she was still feeling tender. 'What would you like to be, son?'

'I don't know. The Eng——' Matt hesitated over the bone of contention, but continued bravely: 'The English teacher says I'm good at composition. He says I'll maybe be a writer yet.'

'A writer? You mean a lawyer?' Sarah's eyes danced with ambitious zeal.

'No. An author.'

'Oh, Matt!' It was so absurd she wanted to laugh. An author! Such nonsense! There weren't any authors among their acquaintances. Even Mrs. M'Cotton had never mentioned such a creature in any of her lists of swell friends. It was one thing to give in to the boy in the matter of leaving school and not becoming a teacher, but it was another matter altogether to let him run away with idiotic ideas. Matt, studying the varying expressions on his mother's face, guessed what she was thinking. He was afraid of that! Oh well! He cleared his throat:

'Maybe I'd better ask Dad to get me into the shipyard,' he blurted out.

Sarah bowed her head to hide her tears. The downcome! Her bonnie wee Matt a common, dirty working man! She sniffed. 'Wait till your father comes back,' she temporized. 'I'll have a talk with him.'

There the matter ended for the time being, but it was only a fortnight later that Matt went off to learn to be a fitter like his father. Another misfit in the scheme of things.

CHAPTER 9

WEDDING BELLS

THE next few years passed quietly enough. Matt had settled down dourly to his apprenticeship, still reading volume after volume of what his mother insisted were trashy novels. One day she picked up one of them and looked at the title: *War and Peace*, she read, by LEO NIKOLAEVICH TOLSTOY. Oh dear—it looked awful Russian—was Matt turning into a Bolshie? But as the days went by, and Matt showed no signs of coveting the soap-boxes she got for firewood from the grocer, Sarah grew easier in mind. Peter, smart lad, was doing well in the Higher Grade—no, she must remember to say Secondary School. Secondary School. Secondary School. He was good at everything, but why, oh why, would he insist on being an engineer instead of a teacher? It seemed to his mother to be a downright waste of good education to go to the university and get B.Sc. after his name and then want to work among dirty machinery. Really! her family had the commonest tastes! Maisie was her mother's only hope. Her childish girniness had grown into an adolescent flair for criticizing everything and everyone—especially the members of her own family. Oh well, maybe she would grow out of that! seventeen wasn't such a decisive age. Certainly she looked like being the beauty of the family.

As for Polly—Sarah sighed every time she thought of her. What a trial the girl was! Always daft on the boys—some of them nice enough—she had finally fixed up with Dick M'Cotton of all people! Sarah would never forget the ache at her heart the night she looked out of the window and saw the two of them at the gate. What a row there had been when Polly had come in and was told she wasn't to be having any carry-on with Mrs. M'Cotton's son. How Polly had tossed her head and said she'd be friendly with him if she liked! And that was where the mistake had been made. If she, Sarah, had taken the thing calmly it might have petered out as so many of Polly's previous affairs

92

had done, but she had gone off the deep end, she admitted to herself. Not that she objected to Dick. Far from it, He was as nice a fellow as you could meet in a day's journey. It was his mother that was the snag.

Always Mrs. M'Cotton had been a thorn in Sarah's flesh. Their husbands had been chums before they were married, and a state of jealousy had existed from the very start. Sarah had felt at first that she had the honours, for she had produced four children to Mrs. M'Cotton's two, but on the other hand Mrs. M'Cotton had had the best of it in having more leisure to sook in with swell folk, as well as having less expense bringing up a family. And Jim M'Cotton had got on—first a clerk, then a cashier with a small firm ; recently there had been rumours that he was being taken into partnership. And now, this ! Polly, headstrong and thwarted, had pushed the friendship for all she was worth, with the result that Mrs. M'Cotton had gone about saying that Polly was throwing herself at Dick, and her not nearly good enough for him. There had been a row over that, of course, but Polly and Dick were by this time so keen on one another that nothing would stop them from getting engaged. That had been six weeks before. Polly was still going about with an air of triumph as ostentatious as the stones in her ring. And now they were talking about getting married ! Dick had a friend in the Housing Department who was keeping an eye on a house for them. To-night Dick was coming up to discuss the wedding arrangements. Oh dear-dear !

Tea over and the table cleared, the younger members of the family went out on their various ploys. Matt, who had no time for girls, went off to the library to change his book. Peter got out his bike from the cellar and bowled away in company with his chums to drive despair into the hearts of motorists on the Stockiemuir Road. Maisie went to the pictures—there was always plenty to criticize there. The only one who seemed unconscious of the importance of the coming discussion was Willie, who sat by the fire smoking and grumbling about what a shame it was he couldn't get out for a walk with Lassie, and it such a fine night.

Polly was on tenterhooks as the minutes went by and Dick still didn't arrive. He had promised to come at seven o'clock, and now it was half-past.

'He'll've ta'en cauld feet,' suggested Willie when the girl for the tenth time asked no-one in particular what was keeping Dick late. Sarah, to whom her husband's colloquialisms were a constant source of humiliation and bewilderment, wanted to know what Dick's feet had to do with it. 'He'll be feart fur the argy-bargy the night!' explained Willie.

'I don't see that there needs to be any argy-bar—ehm—any argument in it!' retorted Sarah.

'Aw, ye'll hae tae gie the chap a chance tae speak 'is mind!' said Willie. 'Ah bet ye he's nae mair in favour o' a big plash nur me.'

Polly, from her post at the window, put a good deal of feeling into, 'Oh, if *he* had his way, we'd be getting married at the dead of night at the bottom of a coal mine.'

'Surely he's no' as ashamed o' ye as a' that!' taunted her father, adding : 'Ah've said it a'readies, an' Ah say it again—Ah don't see whit's wrang wi' gettin' mairrit by the Sheriff. You that works in a Sheriff Officer's—Ah woulda thocht it woulda been the very thing!'

'Don't be ridiculous!' put in Sarah.

'How often have I to tell you, Dad—it's not the Sheriff that marries people! It's the Registrar! You only go before the Sheriff to get a form signed for the registration of the marriage.'

'Well!' demanded Willie. 'Whit's up wi' that?'

With a touch of hysteria Polly left the window and came over to her father, blurting out : 'Sometimes marriage parties have to hang around in a gloomy corridor waiting till the Sheriff's finished with the Criminal Court. . . .'

'Well?'

'Then you go downstairs where your marriage is entered up in the same book as—as—applications to—to disinter bodies and——' Polly gulped. 'And things like that! *So don't say Sheriff to me again!*'

'Ach, keep yer hair on! As Peter says—ye've sure slobbered

a bibful. Ah'm thinkin' ah must be gey glaiket, fur Ah cannae fur the life o' me see *yet* whit that's got tae dae wi' keepin' you f'ae gettin' mairrit by the Sheriff.'

'Don't be so aggravating!' ordered Sarah, but Polly was well equipped by nature for fighting her own battles.

'You don't seem to realize the disgrace!' she stormed. 'Think what the girls in the office would say!'

'Ah don't see ony disgrace! Some o' ma best pals wis mairrit afore the Sheriff!'

'*It's not the Sheriff!*'

'Well, whitever it is! They're as happy the day as some folk that spent a lot o' money——'

'So it's the money that's worrying you!' interposed Sarah, who felt she had been left out of the discussion long enough.

'Naw, it's no' the money—it's this dressin'-up business.' A wheedling note crept into the man's voice as he went on: 'Eh—Polly, would ye no' like jist tae slip across tae the Manse an' get it done there?'

'Oh, don't be silly!' retorted Polly. 'It's—it's heathenish!'

'Hoo can it be heathenish if it's in the Manse?'

To that, Sarah nipped in with: 'There's going to be no hole-and-corner appearance about our daughter's wedding!'

'A weddin' at the Manse doesnae need tae be hole-an'-corner,' Willie gave back. 'Ye could get Peter an' 'is pals tae go roon the doors giein' oot bills, an' ye could get a few hunner sangwidge men tae parade Argyle Street fur weeks aforehand. Only—don't ask me tae dress masel' up in a lum hat an' a frock-coat!'

'There's no frock-coats nowadays,' Sarah pointed out.

'Well, claw-haimmer jaiket, if ye like it better. The very idea! Polly's worried aboot whit the lassies in 'er office wid think if she wis gettin' mairrit afore the Sher—the thingummy, but whit wid the chaps in the work think about me? Ach, as the Clincher used tae say——'

Sarah got in just in time with, 'Willie! For goodness' sake!' while Polly added imploringly, 'Dad! Don't! Not that disgusting expression!'

'Ach!' said Willie, spitting defiantly into the heart of the fire, 'Ah don't know whit things is comin' tae when a man cannae say whit 'e likes in 'is ain hoose!'

Polly had been so intent on the subject of their talk that she had abandoned her look-out post at the window; she was as much startled as delighted, therefore, when the doorbell rang. She got up, saying, 'Thank goodness, that's Dick at last. I'll go to the door.'

Lassie, barking furiously, accompanied her as she ran down the stairs. Dick was a favourite with Lassie. He always carried a peppermint sweetie in the turn-up of his trousers.

'Put on your jacket, Willie!' urged Sarah as the barking retreated.

'Ach, lea'e me alane. Ah'm fine. Ah'm sure Dick's seen shirt-sleeves afore this. Ye'll be askin' me tae pit up ma umberella next!'

Lassie's welcoming bark had suddenly ceased. She returned to the living-room, tail a-droop, and made for her basket, turning round *en route* to throw back a contemptuous growl. But Sarah required no advice from the dog as to the identity of their visitor; instead of Dick, it was his mother. Sarah knew that affected voice too well. In a moment Polly ushered in her future mother-in-law.

'Oh, Mrs. M'Cotton!' said Sarah with cold politeness. 'Come in.'

'Good-evening, everybody!' simpered the new-comer. 'Eh hope Eh'm not intruding. Oh, excuse me! Eh see Mr. McFlehnnel isn't quate dressed yet.'

Sarah drew forward a chair; she was blessed if she would invite the woman to take off her hat and coat. 'Oh, it's all right,' she said. 'He's just like your own husband—he hates sitting around the house with his jacket on. Here—take this chair.'

Mrs. M'Cotton lowered herself into the proffered chair with dignity. That was another thing Sarah grudged her—her figure. While she herself had to suffer miseries of corsetry, here was this woman with her slimness as a constant challenge. Oh, yes!

she thought, I can see the new stone-marten fur tie all right, but I'm going to ignore it—at least as far as saying anything to Mrs. M'Cotton is concerned, but wait till she goes away and I'll give it to Willie for not buying me one before this !

' I wonder what's keeping Dick,' said Polly, going back to the window. ' He's never been so late before.'

Mrs. M'Cotton eased the stone-marten scarf from her shoulders. ' Dick was telling me this morning that there was to be a little—um—discussion to-night about the wedding arrangements, and—well, you see—Eh thought—um—that it might be as well for me to come along too and see that the M'Cottons get a proper consideration.'

Sarah was furious, but Willie got in first with, ' An' whit kinna-like weddin' are *you* on for ? Would ye like us tae book Ham'den Park an' twa-three brass bands ? '

' Oh, be quiet, Willie ! ' said Sarah.

Mrs. M'Cotton, as if she hadn't heard either question or protest, went on : ' Eh was just speaking to meh friend Mrs. McPlush, and she was telling me that the Gigantic Hotel people do weddings awfully well. She was saying——'

' Help ma boab ! ' ejaculated Willie. ' The Gigantic Hotel ! Hae ye ta'en leave o' yer senses or whit ? Here's thae young folk mairryin' intae a wee hoose the size o' a hen-coop, an' ye rave aboot the Gigantic ! '

' Of course, if it's a question of money——' Mrs. M'Cotton hitched the stone-marten back on to the shoulder nearer to Sarah, who rapped out :

' It's nothing of the kind a question of money. It's a question of what's going to be most suitable.'

Mrs. M'Cotton conceded that her son had expressed his determination to have a quiet wedding ; indeed she even went so far as to admit that he had been ' a leetle bit nesty ' about the affair this morning before he went to his work.

' Whit did Ah tell ye ! ' Willie found himself unable to refrain from the taunt. ' The chap's ta'en cauld feet, Polly. So ye may's well come back f'ae the windy.'

' Oh, we'll talk him round all right,' declared the bridegroom's mother. 'What Eh always say is—a woman should start training her man even before they're married, so you'll just have to be firm with him, Polly.'

Polly reflected grimly that this was rather a change of front on the part of her future mother-in-law, but she continued to gaze out of the window, saying, 'I wish he'd come. I hope he hasn't met with an accident.'

'My, ye're jist like yer mother,' said Willie.

'Perhaps you've made up your minds about where it's to be?' queried Mrs. M'Cotton tentatively.

'Well, no, not exactly,' said Sarah. 'We're not sure yet whether to have it in the church, with a reception afterwards.'

'Whit's a reception?' asked Willie, more in alarm than in ignorance.

Sarah made a gesture of annoyance. You could always rely on Willie to open his mouth and put his foot in it. 'You know quite well what a reception is!' she said. 'After the ceremony in the church, everybody goes to a hotel or to the Magnificent——'

'Sarah! Ye're jokin'!' gulped Willie. 'Ye're no' thinkin' o' the Magnificent fur Polly's weddin'?'

'Why not?'

'It's very nice,' commented Mrs. M'Cotton, who, rather than remove her fur, preferred to hitch her chair farther from the fire.

'Why not?' repeated Sarah doggedly.

'Jist because—Ah—Ah couldnae dae it, Serah. Ye wid jist hae tae lea'e me at hame. Ah——' Willie took out his handkerchief and mopped his brow. 'Ah'm jist a workin' man!'

'You're nothing of the kind a working man! You're a foreman!' snapped Sarah.

'Is that your idea o' a joke?' countered Willie. 'A' this talk aboot the Gigantic Hotel and the Magnificent Tea-Room——'

'Restaurant!' The correction came from all quarters.

'Makes me want tae boak!'

'Willie!' Sarah was sick with disgust and exasperation.

'Well, makes me want tae vomit, if ye think that's mair refined. Whit wey can yez no' be content wi' a quiet feed in the

98

hoose here. Jist wursel's an' Dick's folk instead o'—ninety-five folk did ye say it wis, Serah ? '

' I'm surprised at you, Willie ! ' said Sarah. ' Just think what people will say about you being too mean to give your daughter a decent wedding.'

' Ah don't care a docken whit folk say. Whit Ah save on the banquet can go tae help the young folk furnish their hoose.'

At that, Mrs. M'Cotton, in her heat, pulled off the stone-marten and laid it across her knee. ' Dick's quite well able to furnish a house himself ! ' she retorted, with a slight roughening of the varnish of her speech. ' In any case, his own father——'

Willie interrupted her. ' Whit Ah say is this—get the meenister tae come up tae the hoose an' tie the knot here.'

' Oh, Dad, you're hopeless ! ' shouted Polly from the window. ' I've made up my mind I'm going to be married in the church with bridesmaid and——'

This time it was Mrs. M'Cotton who did the interrupting. ' That's right, Polly. What I always say is——'

Then Sarah took her chance to cut in with ' Well, Mrs. M'Cotton, how many relatives do you think we should invite from your side ? '

' Oh, it's not only relatives Eh'm concerned about ! ' The visitor had regained her poise, and her affected speech. ' Eh don't want any of meh special friends left out. Eh want the McPlushes and the McVelvets and the M'Camel Hairs to be there ! '

' I'm not sure if we can extend the invitation beyond relatives,' said Sarah quietly. ' They come first, of course.'

' Not at all ! Some of Mr. M'Cotton's people Eh wouldn't be seen dead with, and these friends Eh'm telling you about are such *awf'lly* nice people, and Eh'm sure they'd give handsome presents.'

' The thought of presents never entered my head ! ' averred Sarah blandly.

' Aw, Serah,' exclaimed Willie, ' d'ye no' mind, jist at tea-time the night——'

To drown her husband's revelations, Sarah plunged hurriedly

99

into : ' Well, supposing we restrict ourselves to a dozen friends on each side, apart from relatives ? '

' Dear me, Mrs. McFlehnnel, surely you don't think Mr. M'Cotton and Eh have only half a dozen friends each ! '

' Oh, if it comes to that, the McFlannels have as wide a circle as you have, but we must draw the line somewhere ! '

' *Well*, Eh must insist on Mr. and Mrs. M'Camel-Hair being there. They're *extra* special friends—they've just fli—ehm—removed to a perfectly *marvellous* house out at King's Park. Not a scheme house, of course. They're *awf'lly* nice people ! '

Before Sarah could reply, Polly squealed with relief and delight, ' Oh, here's Dick at last. He's running.'

' That'll be tae het up thae cauld feet ! ' remarked Willie, but nobody heeded him ; Lassie, barking her welcome, rushed to the door with Polly. Mrs. M'Cotton called after her, ' Well, Polly, we'll just not allow Dick to say one word about a quiet wedding. What Eh always say is—it's entirely the woman's affair.'

To fill in the gap while the door was being opened, Sarah bent down to attend to the fire while Mrs. M'Cotton took the opportunity to lay her fur on Sarah's vacated chair. Dick was in the room so quickly that it must have been a very perfunctory greeting he had given Polly at the door. And judging by Lassie's behaviour, he had also omitted to put the usual peppermint in his trouser turn-up.

' Hullo, Mother, you here ? ' said Dick, breathing heavily. ' Sorry, folks, I'm so late. I had to work on at the office. Such excitement ! It's a long story, but——'

Mrs. M'Cotton cut him short. ' You can tell us all about it afterwards, dear. We're having a nice talk about the wedding arrangements.'

' Oh, but—— ' exclaimed Dick.

Sarah, seeing the fur on her chair, interrupted with, ' You take that seat beside your mother, Dick. I'll sit on the settee.'

' Thanks, but—— '

' Now, Dick, you're not to be tiresome ! ' said his mother. ' It's all fixed up ! '

' But just a minute——'

' Dick ! ' implored Polly. ' Please ! For my sake ! '

' Aw, here ! Let the chap get sayin' 'is piece!' interposed Willie.

' No, we won't ! ' declared Mrs. M'Cotton. ' We're all agreed it's the woman's affair.'

' Oh, can't you let me——' began Dick again, when Sarah put out a restraining hand, saying :

' I think, Dick, if you just allow us to settle the point we were discussing before you came in——'

' But, look here——'

At that Polly burst into tears, wailing, ' Oh, Dick, I never thought you were so selfish. All my life I've wanted a nice wedding, with all my friends round me——'

' Yes, Polly, but you *must* let me explain——'

' Dick ! ' shouted his mother. ' You're carrying on like a spoiled child that always wants its own way.'

The young man was exasperated. He flung his mother's fur unceremoniously in the direction of Lassie's basket and sat down with, ' Oh, you don't understand. I——'

' Yes, Dick,' said Sarah comfortingly, ' I think we do understand, but, after all, if you're as proud of Polly as you seem to be, you should be willing——'

' It's not that, it's——'

' Aw, Dick, gi'e it up ! ' advised Willie, rescuing the carcase of the dead animal from the suspicious attentions of the live one. ' We're bate, right f'ae the very start—there's three o' theym tae two o' us. Come on oot fur a walk.'

' You'll do nothing of the kind ! ' Sarah folded her arms as she watched her husband dither around with the stone-marten tie. He hung it over the back of his chair as she added, ' You'll just sit down again and help us with your advice.'

' Oh, for goodness' sake ! ' yelled Dick. ' Will you let me speak ! '

Said Polly, ' Dick, you're absolutely unreasonable ! Every girl wants a pretty wedding, and I'm sure you'll feel all right about it if you'll only think of *my* point of view for a minute.'

' Yes, but I've got a point of view too ! '

' Be quiet, Dick ! ' ordered his mother. ' We're just not going to listen to you ! '

Which made Dick wild. ' You'll *have* to listen to me ! ' he shouted. ' I tell you——'

' Aw, Dick, ye havenae a chance ! ' said Willie, getting to his feet again. ' Come on oot tae the gairden. A wee spot o' weedin' 'll be a treat by's this collie-shangie ! '

This time Dick appealed to his future father-in-law. ' But, listen——'

' Hold your tongue, Dick ! ' said his mother. ' You're being rude now ! ' Sarah reflected that Mrs. M'Cotton must be very anxious for a big wedding if she would actually rebuke her darling for being rude to ' a common five-eighth ' like Willie McFlannel, but what was the woman saying now ? ' Never heed him, Mrs. McFlannel. What was that you were saying about the number of guests ? '

Before Dick could open his mouth, Sarah rushed in with, ' I said I thought we ought to confine it to relatives and a dozen outside friends on each side.'

This time Mrs. M'Cotton seemed more amenable, so Polly hurried to say, ' I was wondering if Dick's wee cousin could be a train-bearer ? Maisie will be a bridesmaid along with Jenny McLeather.'

' Eh think wee Molly would make a lovely little train-bearer. Perhaps we could get a wee boy the same height, and if they were both dressed in a paler shade than the bridesmaids' frocks——'

' For goodness sake *stop* ! ' shouted Dick furiously. ' You can't go on arranging——'

' I'm surprised at you, Dick—trying to force *your* opinions on us the way you're doing ! ' said Polly.

' Don't you heed him ! ' advised Mrs. M'Cotton.

Dick had got to his feet and was now standing, side-by-side with Willie, in front of the fire. Willie nudged him and whispered, ' Jist you watch this, Dick ! ' He cleared his throat and said aloud, ' Ehm—Ah hope ye're no' forgettin'——'

Both Polly and her mother, in unison, jerked out, ' Oh, don't you start now ! '

But Willie continued unmoved, ' Ah hope ye're no' forgettin'
ma Auld Auntie ! '

There was a gasp of horror. When Sarah had found her voice,
she said, ' I would never *dream*——' while Polly said, ' *She's* not
being invited ! ' and Mrs. M'Cotton : ' That filthy old woman ! '

' Then, if Auld Auntie's no' goin'—neither am Ah ! '

' Willie ! ' reproved Sarah. ' She'll disgrace us ! The way
she dresses ! The way she talks ! '

' And the things she does ! ' contributed Mrs. M'Cotton.
' Why—the other day Eh was hearing that she'd lost an old cup,
and she was down at the midden, poking among the rubbish
for it.'

Willie laughed with relish. ' Ay, she's a great auld caird, is
Auld Auntie. She wis tellin' me no' long ago that she had a lota
claes, but they were a' jaikets ! '

Sarah **was** affronted. ' That's not true ! For I met her last
week in the street, and she made me fair black burning ashamed
of her by lifting her skirt in broad daylight—in the street, mind
you—and showing me a petticoat that belonged to her grandmother ! '

' Well, Ah don't care ! She's ma faither's only sister, an'
bluid's thicker than water. She's got mair right tae be at the
weddin' than a' yer McPlushes an' McVelvets an'——'

Polly went up to her father, grasping him by the sleeve-holes
of his waistcoat, ' Oh, Dad, please ! Please let's have the wedding
without that old woman. I'm sure she'd never enjoy it. She'd
be out of her element.'

' Naw, Polly, ma mind's made up ! Nae Auld Auntie, nae
big weddin'.'

' Speaking for mehself,' interjected Mrs. M'Cotton, ' Eh
would feel black burning shame if meh friends got to know that
Dick was marrying into a fehm'ly with such low-down con-
nections.'

' Noo, mind whit ye're sayin', missus ! ' warned Willie.

Sarah was so angry she could hardly form her words. ' If it
comes to that, Mrs. M'Cotton, you've got nothing to crow about
yourself. Some of us havenae—haven't forgotten the time your

faither—ehm—father flitted a' 'is belongin's on a barrow from the Irish Laun' to——'

'It's a lie!' snapped Mrs. M'Cotton.

'It's no' a lie!'

'Oh, come on out of here, Mr. McFlannel,' said Dick, but Willie, sensing an impending passage at arms, said, 'Naw. Wait. The fun's jist stertin'.'

Polly too seemed to be aware of the forces at work against her schemes, for she cried out, 'Oh dear, can't you forget these old quarrels?'

Mrs. M'Cotton sat back in her chair, planted her heels firmly on the floor and said, 'There's one thing Eh'll never forget, and that's the wey—way—your sister Lizzie treated me the night afore—ehm—before she was married. If *she's* goin', then Ah'm no goin' a step!' The veneer gradually dropped from her speech as she reached the end of her declaration.

Said Sarah, with a similar deterioration, 'An' if that shauchly wee nyaff of a cousin of yours is goin', then Ah'm no' goin' a step eithers!'

'Oh this is terrible,' wailed Polly, trying to catch Dick's eye, but he, like Willie, was too entertained by the dialogue between the two women to heed her.

'He is nut a shauchly wee nyaff!' yelped Mrs. M'Cotton. 'An', anyway, what aboot your Uncle Sammy? We havenae seen *him* fur a gey long while!'

At that, Willie took pity on his wife. 'Heh-heh! That'll dae! Let sleepin' dugs lie! Me an' Dick'll away oot fur a wee dauner. Youse can settle the weddin' business atween yez. Only, mind! Auld Auntie's got tae be there!'

He grasped Dick's arm and led him to the door. The young fellow seemed reluctant to go, and at the door he stopped and whispered something to Willie. Willie gaped at him incredulously, gave a loud guffaw and held out his hand, saying, 'Shake!' Dick shook to the complete mystification of the ladies. 'Come on, Lassie. Oot fur a walk!' added Willie, still grinning broadly. And before the others could demand an explanation they were gone, the dog having flung herself ahead of them in an ecstasy.

An hour later the men returned in time to hear Polly say, ' Well, I think that's everything fixed. I'll see the bridesmaids, if you'll arrange about the wee train-bearer, Mrs. M'Cotton. Dick and I will go and see the minister to-morrow, and we'll get the invitations printed——'

' No, we'll not ! ' said Dick.

The three women immediately began to shriek in exasperation : ' Oh dear, have we to go into it all again ! ' ' Dick, for goodness' sake don't start that ! ' and ' Now, Dick, don't you go and spoil things ! ' Polly added a postscript : ' But, Dick, everything's fixed up. You can't go and upset——'

' Yes, I can. For I'll not be there ! '

His statement had the effect of an explosion. When his mother had recovered, she said, ' Why ? How ? '

' Because I'm going to Canada at the end of the week. One of the chaps in the Toronto branch has left suddenly and they're sending me out. It's promotion. That's why I'd to work late to-night. So the wedding'll have to be in Canada ! '

The three women looked at one another. Said Mrs. M'Cotton, ' You're a mean thing, Dick ! Sitting there all the time and never saying a word ! '

CHAPTER 10

A HOUSE TO LET

DICK sailed at the end of the week—and with Polly's full approval. Once the girl had got over her initial disappointment, she was shrewd enough to see that he was a young man with a future. Seven years from now he might be manager of the Toronto branch—just think of the impression she could make then, compared with the fleeting glory of a big wedding and perhaps having to live in a poky wee house in Croftfoot or Scotstounhill for the rest of their lives. Pf! Scotland was a stodgy country anyway! She would go out to Canada in three months and marry Dick quietly.

As for Sarah, she was at first too wrapped up with the problem of buying Polly's trousseau to feel any regrets, and after that, when the presents began to come in, she had other problems to occupy her mind. There was, to begin with, the incident that took place when Uncle Mattha's present was handed over. It consisted of a jelly dish which caused Sarah to sniff pointedly when it was presented by Mrs. Mattha—a gesture rightly interpreted by that lady, who remarked that if there had been a wedding the gift would, of course, have been more impressive.

'Huh!' said Sarah. 'Look what you're saving not having to buy wedding clothes!'

'Sure, we've got the waddin' clothes already!' retorted Aunt Biddy. 'We got them fur me niece's waddin' in the Spring.'

'Well, look at the taxi fares you've saved!'

To which Aunt Biddy replied that if Sarah didn't want the jelly dish, she would take it away. For a moment Sarah was tempted to say: 'Take it and clear out!' but the memory of Polly's eager counting of the presents kept her back. Polly wanted to surpass the total reputed to have been achieved by a former colleague who had boasted she had received two hundred and three presents. Two hundred and three ! Polly had a long way to go yet, unless she did as Maisie suggested and counted the cutlery as individual items.

The day that Mrs. McLeather arrived with a silver tea service was a memorable one for Sarah.

'Oh, you shouldn't have done that !' she protested as each item came out of its tissue-paper wrapping. 'Oh, what a beauty ! Far, far nicer than Mrs. M'Cotton's. Oh my, what'll Polly say when she sees this ! It's far too kind of you !'

'Oh well,' said Mrs. McLeather, 'our Jenny and Polly have always been such friends, but apart from that, Mr. McLeather and I thought we'd like to do it as much for your sake and Willie's as for Polly's.'

Sarah blinked back a sudden rush of tears. 'That's the nicest thing I've had said to me for years,' she gulped. Life was funny. You got a slap from one direction and a pat from the other. Taken all in all, there were more pats than slaps, for later in the day, when Sarah went to the door and found her old neighbour, Mrs. McTweed, standing there, she wondered if she could be dreaming. And with a present too !

'It's no' much,' declared Mrs. McTweed with her usual candour. 'But Ah jist felt Ah had tae dae somethin' tae—tae make up fur the things Ah used tae say aboot the wee McFlannels. They were wee ladies an' gentlemen compared wi' the trash that's livin' in your auld hoose noo.' And she laid a tablecloth in Sarah's hands.

Even the cross Mrs. McRubber who lived below, and who still insisted that the McFlannels were a noisy crew, shoved a parcel into Sarah's message-crowded arms one day. 'That's a wee mindin' fur Polly !' said Mrs. McRubber. 'She aye smiles sae cheery at ye, ye cannae help wishin' she'll—she'll be happy.' Unwrapped, Mrs. McRubber's present turned out to be another jelly dish, but both Polly and her mother were inordinately proud of it.

Uncle Geordie and his wife came along one evening with a handsome down-quilt that everybody admired until Aunt Polly and her husband turned up with another exactly the same. There was a good deal of acrimony in the discussion that followed as to which of them was to ask the Co-operative Drapery Department to exchange the article. A compromise was finally reached when Willie suggested they should both ask for blankets instead —a proposal Sarah hailed with delight, saying young folk could never have too many blankets. She changed her mind, however, in less than a week when no fewer than six pairs were handed in —over and above the two pairs in dispute and over and above also the two pairs Polly had bought for herself as part of her trousseau and the three pairs that she, Sarah, had laid aside for her since the engagement had been announced.

The day set apart for the show of presents was full of irritations, surprises, and intense exhaustion for the three women most closely concerned, for seventy-three people had pronounced everything to be *lovely*, from the wringer to the mountain of blankets, and even Polly was beginning to tire of the sound of the word. She was, by ten o'clock, incredibly cross, so cross, in fact, that she slapped Peter's face when he gave an impersonation of her going round with the visitors saying, 'And this is from meh Uncle Garge . . . And this is from meh Ehnt Pally. . . .' Maisie, too, disgusted with the smell of stewing tea, sought relief for her feelings by adding to the impersonations. It was all too much for Polly. She burst into hysterical tears and went to bed, leaving all the washing-up to be done by her mother and Maisie. Her dreams were largely composed of a recapitulation of the day's events : 'And this is from. . . .' 'And this is from. . . .' 'And this——' ' Oh, isn't it *lovely* ! ' 'And this frying-pan is from——' ' Oh, isn't it *lovely* ! '

A week later all the excitement was over—Polly was away. So, too, were the packing-cases that had cluttered every room in the house. The last wisp of straw had been swept up, the last hysterical squabble with Polly had been settled, the last kiss exchanged, the last festoon between quayside and boat snapped, the last wave of handkerchiefs. For Sarah, however, there was still a lot to be done. Maisie would now be promoted to Polly's bedroom while Peter would move into Maisie's. To be sure the room was little bigger than a cupboard with a window in it, but the boy was inordinately proud of it. He had recently begun to take an interest in the construction of wireless sets, and his father, to ensure that the family would at least be able to hear the News Bulletins from their own set, gave the boy some money to buy gadgets for himself. The result was that the little room was soon strewn with wires that had a knack of reaching out and tripping you when you were making the bed ; or you would maybe find a thing like an electric bulb under the pillow ; or you would maybe have to rummage beneath a pile of magazines to find what Peter had done with his pair of dirty socks. Sarah was very patient with him, though. She had her own private views on his propensities. Who knows, she thought, what might come out of it ? Why, he might even get a job in the BBC ! Wouldn't that be ever so much better than a dirty engineer ? It was ridiculous to think that he would be able to write B.Sc. after his name and yet go to work like an ordinary workman. And what a chance that would be to boast to Mrs. M'Cotton ! Many a conversation Sarah held in imagination with that lady in front of the kitchenette mirror. It always followed the same lines :

'Oh, good-morning, Mrs. M'Cotton. Have you had a letter from Canada this week ? '

'No. Had you ? '

'Oh, yes. Polly's keeping real well. They've got their house furnished now.'

'That's nice. And how are you all keeping ? '

'Fine, thanks. Peter starts working on Monday.'

'Is that so ? An engineer, of course ! '

'Oh, not an ordinary one. He's joining the staff of the BBC.'

There was always a pause at this point of the imaginary dialogue ; Sarah could never quite make up her mind whether Mrs. M'Cotton's face should register unbelief or pleasure or just plain amazement. Then the conversation would be resumed :

'What's he doing at the BBC ? Is he going to be putting up aerials for people in their back gardens, or something ? '

'Oh, no.' Sarah's reply would always be very casual. 'Oh, no. He's going to learn to be an Announcer ! '

And so it would go on. All this was very much in the future, though. Even Sarah wasn't such a fool as to imagine that the BBC engaged their Announcers at the age of fourteen.

Oh, if only Matt would show some of Peter's needle-like interest in things ! But Matt, still his mother's favourite in spite of his faults, kept on reading his books. Was it possible that Polly had been right when she had said, years ago, that he was nothing but a round O ? Matt's apprenticeship was over now— he was a fully fledged fitter, but he seemed to take no interest in his work. What was worse in Sarah's eyes was the fact that he had no friends—either male or female. There was always something so cutting about what he said about people any time he deigned to take part in the family conversation. Or was ' cutting ' the right word ? Sarah pondered the point. No. It wasn't always cutting, but it was unfailingly, uncannily near the truth, whatever his opinion about people—which raised another thought in the mother's heart. Just recently she had noticed him writing in a wee black notebook. Often, in the middle of a meal, he would brighten up for a second, a smile would glint across his face, and out would come the notebook, down would go a few words, and not all the teasing in the world would break him of the habit. Whatever was he up to ? Sarah felt she would be justified in looking at the book if she ever came across it. After all, who was more interested in a boy's affairs than his mother ? But the wee black notebook never seemed to be lying around.

As for Maisie, every morning she would tear out of the gate, her battered school-case usually under her arm since the handle was almost always loose, and off she would go to her beloved school. She was in the final year now, and was never reluctant to produce the Report Card for her father's signature. And every evening she would come home and wallow in her home lessons. Of course she was going to be a teacher ! She was Sarah's pride and joy. Some day the postman would be pushing letters through the box addressed to ' Mr. Peter McFlannel, B.Sc.' and to ' Miss Maisie McFlannel, M.A.' Oh, Matt, Matt, you're a round O !

Polly had been away about six months when, one evening, Willie came home from his work half an hour later than he ought to have done. He was more bad-tempered than his wife had ever known him. Striding into the living-room, he pitched his soft-felt hat on to the leatherette settee where it lay within an aura of its own dust.

'Ah'm fed up!' he declared. 'D'ye know hoo long Ah had tae wait fur a bus the nicht? Twenty-five meenits! Twenty-five meenits! Is Matt hame yet?'

'Not yet,' answered Sarah, putting the final touches to the tea-table that had been set for three-quarters of an hour. She sighed. Willie was as good as a gramophone record when he got on to the subject of Corporation buses. He had been going on in the same way since ever they came to stay in Knightswood. There was no reason why to-night should be any exception. Even Lassie seemed to be aware that when her beloved master was in this mood it was no time to go forward with a ball in her mouth. As Sarah suspected, the monologue followed its usual lines.

'This place is at the backa beyond! Ah'm fed up wi't. Ah'll catch ma daith o' cauld staunin' doon there at Partick Cross waitin' fur a bus. Ye can get caurs fur Dalmuir—hunners o' them. Ye can get buses fur Maryhill—hunners o' them. Ye can get steam-lorries an' horse-lorries an' bikes, but ye can never get a bus goin' tae Knightswood! Ah'm fed up! Naw! don't gi'e me ma tea the noo. Wait tae Ah get het up a bit. Ah'm freezin'! Twenty-five meenits! Says Ah tae the conductor when it came alang, "Heh, are you tryin' races wi' Halley's Comet, or whit?" Here! Fur peety's sake gi'e's somethin' tae eat. Ah'm perished. Twenty-five meenits!'

And so it went on. And on. By-and-by Matt came in and announced that he had had to walk all the way home.

Said Willie, 'It jist comes tae this—we'll hae tae flit! Back tae Partick Road. Ah'm no' gettin' ony younger. Ah'm no' fit fur this kinna life—cairried meals an' waitin' fur buses hour efter hour.'

As this announcement was also quite according to schedule,

Sarah paid no attention to it, but when Matt said that he, too, was fed up, she leaned forward :

' Now, Matt—don't say *you* want to go back to Partick Road ! '

' Well, it would be a good bit nearer the Library for me ! '

' Huh ! ' said Maisie with a sneer, ' why don't you put up a bed there ? '

' Jolly good idea ! ' exclaimed Peter. ' Let's go back to Partick Road and I can have the Place on the Stair for a lab'ratory ! '

' Peter,' warned Sarah, ' don't be vulgar ! ' Really ! The things these young folk said ! If they came away with that in their own homes, what would they say outside ? Sarah blushed for Peter, who was now explaining to Maisie that if she couldn't see the pun she was pretty stupid. After that the discussion became an argument over the correct pronunciation of the word ' laboratory.' In a little while, though, Willie brought the subject back to its starting-point.

' Well, if ye're a' too stuck-up fur tae go back tae Partick Road, whit aboot lookin' fur a hoose in some other street off Dumbarton Road ? Ah'm sure there's lots o' hooses wi' inside closets thonder.'

' Willie,' protested Sarah, ' don't you be vulgar now ! '

' It's all right, Mother ! ' soothed Peter, ' the word's in the Bible, you know ! '

' And don't you be irreverent ! ' snapped his mother. Dear-dear ! No wonder Mrs. M'Cotton could cultivate swell friends ! She hadn't a family that gave her a red face every time they spoke. And as for a husband ! ' Willie ! ' she said. ' I'm telling you flat ! I'm not going back to Partick ! '

' Well, whit aboot Whiteinch ? '

But Sarah turned up her nose at that too.

' Hyndland's not too far away for you, Dad,' remarked Maisie.

' Ah'll " Hyndland " ye ! ' stormed her father. ' Ye've got tae be a bank clerk or a retired grocer tae stey thonder ! '

' Are you forgetting that your family's getting on in the world ? ' Sarah was goaded into demanding.

'Whit! Whaur are they? Matt here is jist a common five-eighth. Aren't ye, son?'

But Matt was away in a world of his own. Suddenly he reached for his pocket, drew out the little black book, and wrote something in it. Sarah, under pretext of pouring out more tea for him, caught a glimpse of what he was writing. She could only make out the word 'common' with two figures after it, one on top of the other. What did it mean? The book was back in his pocket in a second.

'Well, anyway, Maisie's going to be a teacher!' said Sarah, 'and maybe Peter'll be working in the BBC yet!' She regretted the words the moment they were uttered, but it was too late to take them back now.

Peter's laugh was at the hooting stage. 'BBC?' he snorted. 'Oh, Mother! Because I'm always stooging around with wireless doesn't mean I'm interested in broadcast entertainment!'

'Who said the BBC were entertaining?' sneered Maisie, and in a minute or two Willie felt he had once again lost control of the situation.

'It's jist like this!' he shouted, thumping the table as he spoke. 'Serah! you and me's goin' oot on Saturday efternune fur a walk. No, Lassie! Doon! Ah didnae mean that kinna walk. We're gonnae hike through the streets tae we come tae a place that's genteel anuff fur ye. . . .'

'Houses to let, of course, grow on trees,' interposed Maisie.

'If ye'd let me feenish whit Ah wis sayin'——'

'Well, we're not going Partick way!' declared Sarah.

'We're goin' Partick wey!' There was a new grimness about his mouth that his wife hadn't noticed before. The buses must really have been extra bad to-night, she thought. By Saturday, though, he would have forgotten all about the fuss he had made. They were perfectly happy at Gartnavel Crescent. And anyway, supposing they went back to a tenement, where would Lassie play herself? She put the question to Willie.

'Lassie'll be a'right up a close! She's steyed up one afore. Sure ye'd like fine tae go back tae Partick Road, Lassie?'

Lassie bounced her agreement, delighted that she was being

taken notice of. Willie and she, as usual, understood each other perfectly.

Long before Saturday afternoon, however, Sarah was won over to Willie's viewpoint, with the assistance of Mrs. McRubber, the woman who lived below them. On Tuesday she came up for the loan of Sarah's carpet sweeper and stayed talking at the door for half an hour. On Wednesday she returned the borrowed article, and, Maisie having gone to the door, Mrs. McRubber asked to see her mother and so got inside. Once seated in the cosy living-room she chattered for almost an hour. The following day she met Sarah on the garden path and pleaded with her to come into her house and see the new carpet she had bought, and before Sarah could get away she had to accept a cup of tea she didn't want. On Friday, though, the climax was reached. When her doorbell rang, Sarah lay doggo, having heard the squeak of Mrs. McRubber's door a few moments earlier. The affair was assuming the proportions of a persecution now—all because they had been civil to her when she had given Polly a wedding present. The doorbell rang again, though. And again. It's no use, thought Sarah. She must know I'm in. She'll have heard me moving about. So the door had to be opened.

' Oh, Mrs. McFlannel,' gushed the woman, ' I'm awful sorry if I've come at an awkward time. Was you in the bathroom ? '

Sarah said ' Mn,' which could mean anything. She kept her hand on the door handle.

' Ma daughter's jist arrived unexpected. I told 'er I'd bring ye down to see the baby.'

' Oh—ehm—I think I've a cold coming on. I'm staying in the house to-day.' Sarah sniffed by way of circumstantial evidence.

' Well, I'll bring them up ! Oh, it's the bonniest wee boy ye ever seen. We'll be up in a minute ! '

Sarah stood gaping after her disappearing neighbour. What impiddence ! What earthly interest had she in the grandchild ? And to think of her bringing it up here ! Really ! But since it was impossible to shut the door in their faces, Sarah was forced not only to invite the women in but also to give them a cup of tea. It was all very well being neighbourly, but this was the limit !

As a result she was ready for the road the following afternoon long before Willie was dressed. They must get out of Gartnavel Crescent before that Mrs. McRubber and she started getting hats the same.

They got the bus to Anniesland Cross. Going down Crow Road in a tramcar, Sarah indicated the fine red sandstone erections *en route*.

Willie made a wry face. ' Naw ! ' said he. ' Thae oriel windaes is too big. Hooses like thur is fur Corporation officials. Yer man wid gi'e ye a rid face there, an' Ah'm ower auld tae learn tae speak pan loaf ! '

The tram trundled to the foot of Crow Road, where they got off and stood, for a moment or two, undecided about which way to turn. Said Sarah, ' Mind you—anything less than a four-room-and-kitchen's no use ! '

' Whit ! ' gulped Willie. ' A four-room-and-kitchen ! Ye're haverin' ! Look—Matt an' Peter in the pawrlur bedplace, Maisie in the bedroom, an' you'n me in the kitchen bed the same as in Partick Road. *Two*-room-and-kitchen ! '

' Do you realize that Peter's going to be doing a lot of study ? He'll need a room to himself. You're not going to spoil his career by scrimping a room for him ! '

Willie hummed and hawed. ' Well — three-room-and-kitchen ! Nae mair ! '

' That means that Matt—the eldest—has got to pig it in the parlour bedplace, while the younger ones get a room to themselves.'

' Well, gi'e Peter the pawrlur—a' the mair room fur'm tae mess aboot wi'.'

' The very idea ! And leave me with no place to show visitors into ! '

' Whit's up wi' the kitchen ? '

Everything was up with the kitchen, but it was no use trying to explain that to Willie in his present mood. She tried other tactics. ' See here, Willie—in a wee while we'll be having our silver wedding——'

' D'ye tell me that ! Ah don't feel a day aulder nor seeventy-nine ! '

' I wouldn't be at all surprised if Polly came home for the occasion. By that time she'll be used to having things a bit better than—than—well, a bit better.'

But Willie saw through that one too, and it fared no better than its predecessor. ' Ye're a great wee lass, Serah, but yer highfalutin' notions run away wi' ye. We're lookin' fur a three-room-and-kitchen hoose. Come on—up this side-street.'

They went up quite a few side-streets that afternoon ; there were lots of boards out advertising six- and seven-room-and-kitchen houses to let, but none the size they, or rather Willie wanted. They were getting nearer and nearer to Byres Road, and Sarah was getting nearer and nearer to despair ; only the memory of the persistent Mrs. McRubber kept her courage from flagging altogether. At last, on the fringes of Dowanhill they caught sight of a dejected notice-board from which a tattered ' To let ' advertisement dangled. Three rooms and kitchen. With a faint recognition of the fact that here they would be fairly near the university for Maisie and Peter, Sarah trudged up the stairs. They got the key from the people next door; hesitatingly they went in.

Everything was very dirty ; clearly it had been lying empty for a long while, but the rooms were big and the outlook open. Immediately Sarah's drooping spirits revived. She was a born home-maker, and she could see possibilities in the place which had obviously escaped other viewers. The sitting-room had a large bed-place as well as a cupboard ; there were, in fact, lots of cupboards. The kitchen, though, was pretty dreary.

' If we got an interior grate in here, we could make this into quite a nice living-room,' said Sarah. ' With the bed-settee in the recess here——'

' Bed-settee yer granny ! ' snapped Willie. ' Ah'm no' sleepin' on thon thing again ! Of a' the instruments o' torture ! Ah tell ye whit—pit it in the sittin'-room fur Peter an' he can use the bed-place fur his labora—ehm—thingmy.'

' Oh, Willie, you don't want to go back to the old-fashioned idea of a bed in the kitchen again, do you ? '

' Ah div that ! Ah wid even plump fur a feather bed if Ah thocht we could buy yin.'

Oh, what's the use of trying to make things nice, thought Sarah. With Willie in that thrawn mood she would just have to bide her time and make changes slowly. They went round the house again. Once it was cleaned up. . . .

The factor refusing to do anything to the house beyond necessary repairs, Willie had to dig pretty deeply into his pocket to defray the expenses of the painters and decorators. After that, Sarah and a charwoman did the cleaning up between them, and the furniture-removers did the rest. The flitting was conducted with the dignity and silence of a funeral, and Peter was delighted with the arrangement that he should sleep on the folding divan-bed in the sitting-room and have the bed-recess for his ' lab ' as he called it. Matt was quite content with the smaller of the two bedrooms, and Maisie was enchanted with the whole situation. She told the girls at school that she was leaving to go to Hyndland School, now that they were living ' in the west end.' Sarah, too, felt that in moving back to a tenement—no, she must remember to call it a flat—the McFlannels had stepped up in the social scale. The neighbours were all such quiet, reserved people, too ! That was all to the good. The washing-house key? Oh, no—she was sending everything—well, nearly everything— to the laundry. Huh—so much for Mrs. M'Cotton should she ask.

As for Willie, he bore with his wife's raptures as patiently as he could. All he cared about was that they were now living nearer his work. He could come home for dinner—which he did in spite of the fact that he was being constantly reminded that none of the other men in the ' close ' did so. There was an open space of ground quite near where Lassie could be exercised, and Kelvingrove Park was near enough for a Saturday afternoon's walk, even though Lassie did have to be put on the leash. Like Willie, Lassie was putting on weight with advancing years. Still and all, life was just fine.

CHAPTER 11

PINPRICKS

SARAH sighed with relief when she heard Willie's key in the door. 'There you are at last!' she exclaimed as soon as he came into the kitchen.

Willie stared around him. 'What wey's the tea no' set?' he demanded.

'Because we're going to the M'Cottons for our tea. Do you not remember?'

'Ach theym! They're aye askin' us up fur wur tea!'

'They are not! We haven't been there since Polly got married. Now, hurry up and get dressed!'

'But ah'm hungry! Can ye no' gie's a wee cuppy tea in wur haun'?' His tones were wheedling.

'I will not! And ruin your appetite for the big feed Mrs. M'Cotton's sure to have, just to show off how much better she can do than me? See—' she added, jerking her thumb in the direction of the door, 'there's Peter out of the bathroom.'

'Is he goin' an' a'?' queried Willie.

'Of course—and Maisie too. She's in the sitting-room looking out some music.'

Willie groaned. 'Music! Help ma boab, is it tae be yin o' thae kinna nichts? Ah could enjoy masel' better at hame wi' the toothache.'

Sarah, realizing that a little cajoling would be necessary, pointed out that she had laid out all his clean clothes, but Willie, refusing to co-operate, or at any rate deciding to make capital out of the situation, assured her he could get ready a lot quicker if he had a cup of tea to egg him on ; he even added the observation that he could take the egg forbye. Sarah, however, declined to take the hint.

'Look,' she said, '—here's your new shirt with the collar to match.'

' Ah hope ye've ta'en oot a' the peens.'

' Of course ! What do you take me for ? '

' For better or worse ! ' cried Willie, seizing her in the bye-going and holding her tight. ' For richer or poorer, to have and to hold——'

' Willie ! ' shrieked Sarah, struggling to get free and yet not struggling very fiercely. ' Stop your nonsense ! You're squeezing the breath out of me ! '

' D'ye no' mind ye promised tae love, honour, and obey me ? '

' Willie ! Come on—let me go. You've no time to waste canoodling ! '

He tightened his grip. ' Did ye, or did ye no'—promise tae obey me ? '

' I——'

' Come on ! '

' Well, I suppose I did ! Oh, you're hurting me ! '

' Make me a cup o' tea then. Ye widnae like me tae disgrace ye by eatin' like a horse at the M'Cottons ? '

In order to facilitate the making of the tea, Willie released his hold ; Sarah, placing herself strategically safe behind the table, told him that he would enjoy his tea all the more when he got to the M'Cottons if he went with an empty stomach. ' We're late as it is,' she added so convincingly that Willie took off his jacket with a resigned, if disgusted snort. Sarah was quick to follow up her advantage.

' Do hurry ! ' she pleaded. ' You know how the M'Cottons are always here long before the time when they're invited for tea. See—here's your suit. You can change in the bathroom.'

Willie accepted the suit with the remark to no-one in particular that he was suffering in the cause of Bonnie Scotland, and went off to the bathroom saying : ' Mind, if ye havenae ta'en a' the peens oota this new shirt Ah'll—Ah'll make a cuppy tea tae masel' !'

He had snibbed the bathroom door when Maisie came into the kitchen with a pile of music, saying : ' Look, Mother, will these do ? " The Blue Danube Waltz," and I think I could manage some of these preludes.'

' Preludes ? ' Sarah looked at the music doubtfully, then,

catching sight of the composer's name, she added : ' Oh—
Choppin ? Oh, not that, Maisie—it sounds awful sort of cheap.
What about "The Robin's Return "—isn't that the one you cross
your hands at ? '

' Yes, but crossing the hands doesn't increase the value of a
piece of music, Mother ! '

Sarah looked at her daughter dubiously. The girl, now that
she was at the university, was more than ever given to correcting
people, particularly her parents, but on the other hand if she, as
her mother, didn't want to make a fool of herself in front of
Maisie's friends, she would be better to make use of all the advice
she could pick up. Still, she could always make a verbal protest
of opinion. ' Well,' she said, ' I always like to see a pianist
crossing her hands. It looks real professional.'

' Mother ! ' said Maisie with mock patience, ' that's a delusion
worthy of Mrs. M'Cotton.' At that moment Peter came into
the kitchen, and Maisie turned her attention to him. ' Huh ! '
she sneered. ' Here's Peter—and with his long trousers on
too ! '

Peter, self-conscious enough as it was, blushingly informed
his mother that the collar he was carrying was too tight for him.

' And would you look at his hair ! ' went on Maisie. ' You'd
think it was varnished ! ' She sniffed. ' What's the stink ?
Are you trying to catch Jean M'Cotton by the nose ? '

Peter, aware that he had spent a great deal of time on his hair,
tried to side-track the issue by demanding to know who Jean
M'Cotton was.

' Listen to him, Mother ! Trying to kid us on he doesn't
write notes to the girl at school.'

' I do *not* write notes to any girl at school ! ' insisted the
writhing Peter.

' If it wasn't so well plastered down, I'd tell you to keep your
hair on.'

' That'll do, Maisie ! ' interposed Sarah. Turning to Peter
she told him she thought he was looking very nice in his new
long trousers.

' Yes ! ' continued Maisie, undaunted. ' Wait till Mrs.

M'Cotton sees you ! She'll say, " Hullo, Petah, what a big boy you're getting ! Quate a young mehn, in fehct." '

Seeing the misery on the lad's face, Sarah ordered Maisie to go immediately and put in some practice on the pieces of music with which she intended entertaining the company at the M'Cottons' house, ' because,' she added, as the girl moved towards the door, ' I don't want you to make a fool of yourself to-night.'

' She can do that without playing the piano, Mother ! ' retorted Peter, a remark that fetched Maisie swinging back with a retaliation, but her mother got in first with :

' That's enough, you two ! Away you go to the piano, Maisie.' There was something in her mother's voice that made Maisie obey without demur as Sarah continued, ' Now let me see that collar, Peter.'

Peter handed over the article in question. ' I think,' he whispered in self-reproach, ' I've another pimple coming at the back of my neck.'

His mother nodded understandingly, and, while she pulled and tugged at the collar to stretch it, the strains of the piano came filtering from the sitting-room. If Maisie's interpretation were to be believed, the Blue Danube was a very bumpy river.

Half an hour later the four of them stood outside the M'Cotton bungalow. Matt had been excused on the grounds that he had another appointment. Sarah hoped she would not be pressed for details, for Matt's appointment was with a chair in the reading-room of the Partick branch of the Corporation Library.

' Ring the bell, Peter,' said she, ' although I'm sure they must have seen us coming up the path.'

As Peter rang the bell, his father expressed the hope that it would not be cold meat for tea as he was famishing. He further stated that he would not care to be trusted with the task of dishing out ham and egg to the company, no, nor even that least desirable item on his personal menu—fish custard.

' Shsh, Willie ! ' ordered Sarah, adding in an undertone, ' I don't think I'd like one of these clear-glass doors—people can see right into your lobby.'

'Hall, Mother!' corrected Maisie, true to form. 'They don't have lobbies in bungalows.'

Before Sarah could express her opinion about bungalows in general, Willie ordered Peter to ring again in case they hadn't heard him the last time.

'Cheer up, Dad,' exclaimed Peter, his finger to the bell-push, 'they're out! We've come the wrong night!'

'Don't say that! Ah couldnae wait tae Ah got hame again fur ma tea.'

'I'm sure this is the night,' said Sarah dubiously. 'This *is* Thursday, isn't it!' Before she had finished, Mrs. M'Cotton's genteel figure was seen coming towards them, her hand outstretched to open the door.

'Oh, there you all are!' she exclaimed in her edgy, genteel voice. 'Come away in! I didn't hear you the first time you rang.'

Peter, too young to be diplomatic, started out to ask how she knew they had rung twice, but his question was drowned in the torrent of Mrs. M'Cotton's welcome.

'Come away. Maisie. I see you've brought your music. Thet's fehn. Oh, good-evening, Mr. McFlehnnel. Come away —Mr. M'Cotton's just ready. Dear me, Peter, what a big boy you're getting! Quate a young man in fact!' Maisie's significant clearing of her throat was also unheard as Mrs. M'Cotton shouted into the distance, 'Jim! Come and look after Mr. McFlehnnel and Peter!' She turned to her guests again : 'Thet's one benefit of Mr. M'Cotton wirking in an office—he's always dressed. Jim! Oh—here he is!'

Jim M'Cotton, a tall, heavily built man, with a knack of knowing what a girl's ankles looked like before he saw her face, came forward with a hearty manner. 'Here we are—here we are! Well, Willie, how are you to-night? 'Evening, Mrs. McFlannel—and Maisie! Goodness, Peter, what a height you're growing! You'll soon be bigger than your father, but,' he added with a snigger, 'that's not saying much, is it—eh, Willie? Well, I see you've got your coats hung up, so come away into the lounge.'

As the three men disappeared, Mrs. M'Cotton conducted Sarah and Maisie to a bedroom for the purpose of what she described as ' taking off their things,' and also for the purpose of showing off the recent work of an interior decorator. Willy-nilly the two guests had to admire the result until Mrs. M'Cotton exclaimed :

' Oh, Eh'll take your coats. Don't put them on the bed—they might soil the new quilt and bedspread. Jim got them through his firm. They're the very best that could be got—and the latest style. Aren't they gorgeous ! '

Sarah and Maisie agreed, with a regrettable lack of enthusiasm which Mrs. M'Cotton, wrapped as she was in the mantle of her own superiority, failed to notice. Expressing the hope that the coats had tabs on them, she hung them at the back of the bedroom door without troubling to use the tabs. ' Our Jean's wirking late to-night,' she went on, ' and she'll not be home till heff-pest eight, so Eh thought we wouldn't have our supper till then. Jim and I had a cup of tea before you came. Well, if you're ready, Mrs. McFlehnnel ? '

Trying not to show her dismay at the prospect of a half-past eight supper for her hungry husband, Sarah temporized with, ' Just a minute till I see if my hair's right.'

' Oh, you'll do ! ' conceded Mrs. M'Cotton off-handedly. ' Nobody'll worry if it *is* in a mess. Eh had mehn done last week. Mrs. McVelvet put me in touch with her hairdresser. You ought to try her, Mrs. McFlehnnel—Eh'm sure her treatment would help thet dead look your hair's got. Of course, this woman's *frehtfully* expensive ! '

Indignantly Maisie defended her mother, saying, ' Your hair's fine, Mother—as usual. See, give me your net and I'll put it in my handbag.'

Handing over the hair-net, Sarah indicated a small parcel lying on the dressing-table, explaining that it was a cake she had baked for Mrs. M'Cotton.

' Oh,' exclaimed that lady, ' don't leave it on the dressing-table—it might be greasy ! ' She picked it up and left the room, saying, ' You needn't have troubled, you know. Eh've got plenty stuff and Eh always buy the best. Excuse me while I put this in the scullery.'

Instantly Sarah reached out a hand to her daughter. 'Maisie !' she wailed, 'what'll your father say when he finds out about the supper not being till half-past eight. He'll be mad at me !'

'Could you not stage a faint or something so's to get home right away ?' suggested Maisie.

But before they could enter into detailed plans of action, Mrs. M'Cotton was with them again, urging them into the small apartment that she euphemistically called The Lounge. As they entered, Mr. M'Cotton exclaimed :

'Here you are ! Come-away-come-away. Here's the very chair for you, Mrs. McFlannel.'

Sarah looked at the chair and protested that those low tubs were no use for her.

'And how right you are !' said the hostess. 'With your short fat legs it's never very dignified, is it ? Here's a basket-chair for you—Mr. McFlehnnel, won't you have a seat ?'

'Ach, it's no' worth while sittin' doon !' said Willie. 'We'll be goin' ben fur wur——'

Before he could plunge her into complete disgrace, Sarah chopped into the middle of his speech to point out that he was keeping the fire away from everybody else by standing in front of it. Meanwhile Mrs. M'Cotton was urging Maisie to take the piano-stool.

'The piano's just been tuned,' she added, 'so it'll be a treat for you to play.'

Maisie, determined to give as good as she got, said that their piano was tuned twice a year.

'Oh,' said Mrs. M'Cotton, 'but this is a really superior piano. It doesn't need all that tuning.'

At that moment Willie let out a sudden yell. A tiny pin that had escaped Sarah's eye when opening out his new shirt had stung him as he edged his way back to the fire.

'Willie !' exclaimed his wife. 'What's wrong ?'

'Ah'm fine !' he lied. 'Jist lea'e me alane.'

'Here's a fine comfortable seat for you, Willie,' said Mr. M'Cotton indicating a luxurious armchair, but Willie declined it in favour of a small one whose nobbles would be no temptation to lean against. The pin nipped him again as he sat down, but although he stifled his groan Sarah heard him.

'Willie, that's terrible!' she exclaimed. 'Have you a pain somewhere?'

'You mind yer ain business,' he snapped, valiantly resolving not to expose her inefficiencies before her lifelong enemy. Then, seeing Maisie take her seat facing the piano, he added in consternation, 'Maisie's no' gonnae play a choon the noo, is she?'

'Yes,' said Mrs. M'Cotton. 'Come away, Maisie, we're waiting.'

'But I don't want to play if Dad isn't well!'

'Ah'm fine!' insisted Willie, 'but don't make it a long yin.'

'Can I take all these ornaments off the piano, Mrs. M'Cotton?' asked Maisie, only half-assured.

'Dear me—can't you play without all thet fuss?'

'I need to get the music stand out!'

At that Mr. M'Cotton leapt obligingly to his feet. 'I'll help you, Maisie!' he said eagerly. He had had time to discover that 'girning Maisie,' as she had always been known in the M'Cotton household, had now grown up to be a very presentable young lady with an exceedingly neat ankle. His wife observed his eagerness with a placid eye; it never occurred to her that she had anything to fear from the charms of other women, other women having no charms equal to her own.

'What are you going to play?' she asked.

'Play "The Blue Danube," Maisie,' suggested Sarah.

'What about "The Robin's Return"?' counter-suggested the hostess. 'Mrs. McTapestry plays it beautifully. Crosses her hands too.'

'Oh, but crossing the hands doesn't increase the value of a piece of music,' quoted Sarah, confident that Maisie was too absorbed with Mr. M'Cotton's attentions to hear her.

'Will that do now, Maisie?' that gentleman was asking

skittishly. 'My, you've fairly grown up since I saw you last! Quite the young lady! I hear you're at the Uni, too.'

Having no taste for bald, middle-aged men, Maisie replied coldly that she was in her third year—at the Varsity. Mr. M'Cotton, choosing to ignore her different contraction of the word 'University,' went on to ask if she was going to be a teacher, eh?

'Mn,' said Maisie non-committally. 'Well, here's "The Blue Danube"!'

'Oh,' exclaimed Mrs. M'Cotton in disappointment. 'Can you not play "The Robin's Return"? Of course, it's probably too difficult for you——'

'But I *can* play "The Robin's Return"!'

'Thet's very nice,' was the condescending response, so while Mr. M'Cotton took his seat again, and while Maisie plunged half-heartedly into "The Blue Danube," Mrs. M'Cotton proceeded to entertain Sarah. 'Did I tell you,' she began, 'about Jean's latest craze? You remember she wanted to be a nurse?'

Before Sarah had time to reply, Mr. M'Cotton's booming voice was heard asking Willie if he would have a cigar; Willie, reaching forward to accept, let out a yelp that called forth a dismayed appeal from his wife that he would tell her what was the matter. Was it his stomach?

'Naw—it's ma back,' he conceded.

'Is it lumbago?' asked Mr. M'Cotton, preparing to give some first-hand advice.

'Naw—it's no' lumbago!'

'Perhaps it's your kidneys!' said Mrs. M'Cotton. 'Although Eh've always heard it said thet the wirst kehnd of kidney trouble doesn't have any pain.'

Willie, however, assured her solemnly that it wasn't his kidneys.

'Ye've maybe been standing in a draught,' suggested Mr. M'Cotton with a leer. 'You should be ashamed of yourself, Willie—at your age!' Turning to Sarah, he asked if she couldn't keep an eye on her man.

Ignoring the pleasantry, Sarah expressed the opinion that if Willie stood with his back to the fire the heat would relieve the pain.

'Ach,' said Willie, trying to sound off-hand, 'it'll maybe go away when we go through fur wur——'

'Oh, Mrs. M'Cotton,' said Sarah quickly, 'you were telling me about Jean?'

'Oh, yes! Well, she's decided against nirsing after all. She wants to take up hendicrefts.'

'You mean—work in a factory?'

'Good gracious no! The School of Art! It's very expensive, of course. . . .'

At that point Mr. M'Cotton, probably feeling he couldn't bear to hear the tale again, called on Peter to come away from his seat at the window and join the company. Willie, adding his voice to the request, did so with rather too much vigour; as a result he yelped once again as the pin pricked him on what was now a very tender spot.

'Willie!' declared Sarah, 'we'll need to go home if you're as bad as all that! What do you think it can be?'

'Ach, Ah'll go hame efter we've had wur tea.'

'Eh'm gled you haven't hed your tea yet anyway,' put in Mrs. M'Cotton, 'or you meght be blaming me for meh cooking.'

'Speaking about pains in your stomach, Willie,' said the host, 'did you ever hear the story about the wee chap that was crying in the street and his mother ran out to see what was wrong. "Oh," says he, "I've got a pain in my tummy! That other boy kicked me." So his mother turns to the other boy and says, "Why did you kick my little boy in his tummy?" "Well," says he, "he shouldn't have turned round."'

For a moment Willie didn't see the point of the story, but when he did he guffawed, or rather he started to guffaw, but had scarcely achieved his objective when the pin got him again and his mirth was turned to mourning in the same breath.

Sarah was distraught, but Mrs. M'Cotton could only say with disdain that she couldn't see anything to laugh at.

'All I can see,' said Sarah, 'is my husband's face. He must

be in terrible pain. I think we'd better away home and get the doctor.'

'Ah'm no' needin' nae doctor!' insisted Willie.

'Eh could give you cehstor oil, if you liked,' proposed Mrs. M'Cotton with a giggle.

Lifting a very fancy cushion, Sarah advanced on Willie and was preparing to stuff it down behind him in an attempt to ease his pain when she was warned off very thoroughly.

'Have you injured your spine, d'you think?' asked Mr. M'Cotton.

'Naw, it's no' ma spine!'

'Perhaps it's sciatica!' decided Mrs. M'Cotton with an air of satisfaction. 'Eh've a friend who's been lehing in a plehster cehst on the fleht of her beck for weeks. Would you like to leh down? This settee has a drop-end—the very latest. Look, Mrs. McFlehnnel!'

'Ah'm tellin' ye!' Willie shouted before Sarah required to take any notice of the wonderful settee, 'Ah'm fine—or Ah will be when Ah've had ma——'

Before he could say the word 'tea,' Sarah dived into conversation again with all the fervour of one who is really interested in the question on hand: 'Oh, Mrs. M'Cotton, what was that you were saying about your Jean and the factory?'

'I told you,' declared Mrs. M'Cotton in justifiable exasperation, 'it's not a factory—it's the School of Art!'

'Oh, yes, of course.'

'She's very friendly with Margaret McTapestry, you know, and the two of them do everything together.'

It appeared as though Mr. M'Cotton, having heard this particular monologue of his wife's before, wanted to escape hearing it again. With a loud voice he asked Peter if he would have a cigar now that he was into long trousers and all that.

'No, thanks,' said Peter. 'I'm not allowed to smoke.'

'No? Ha-ha—I'll bet you've had a wee puff up the chimney when your mother wasn't looking—eh?'

'Not yet, Mr. M'Cotton.' The redness of Peter's face might

have been due to embarrassment, on the other hand it might equally have been due to the tightness of his collar.

'Well, come on,' wheedled the host, 'you'll never learn younger, and you'll be a man before your mother. Here—take one!'

'Naw, ye'll no'!' cried Peter's father, with such fervour that the pin got to work again, causing a fresh outbreak of yelping.

'Willie, come on away home!' pleaded Sarah.

'But we cannae go withoot gettin' wur tea first! It widnae be fair tae Mrs. M'Cotton efter hur goin' tae a' the bother.'

'But if you're ill?'

'Ah'm no' ill!'

'Then why are you groaning and yelping like that?'

In anxiety to be of some assistance, Mr. M'Cotton said, 'Willie, d'you mind I used to be a stretcher-bearer in 1916? I could give your back a spot of massage.'

'Oh, naw-naw! Oh—the very thocht o't gi'es me jip.'

'Is it only when you move that you feel the pain?'

'Ay.'

'Then it's muscular rheumatism!' declared Mrs. M'Cotton, speaking as one in authority. 'And there's nothing better for that than massage. And a course of acetic acid.'

Willie protested gingerly but with emphasis that he was not suffering from muscular rheumatism.

'Maybe it's wind — ehm — flatulence?' suggested Mr. M'Cotton. 'Sometimes a good thump right on the spot——'

'Aw, don't *suggest* sichna thing! Ach, lea'e me alane, folks. Ah'll be a'right when Ah've had ma——'

Leaping into the emergency once more, Sarah burst out, 'Where were you thinking of going to for your holidays this year, Mrs. M'Cotton?'

In an atmosphere of sudden stillness Mrs. M'Cotton replied, 'Oh, the McTapestrys are talking about the Lake District and we thought we meht go with them.' Suddenly she realized there was no longer any need to shout, for Maisie had stopped playing the piano. 'Go on, Maisie,' she said. 'You're doing very nicely!'

'What's the use of playing when nobody's listening?' demanded the pianist.

'Oh, but we *were* listening! Eh always think music's so nice. So genteel! Don't you, Mrs. McFlehnnel? And I *do* love "The Robin's Return."'

'That wasn't "The Robin's Return,"' replied Maisie without turning round. 'It was "The Blue Danube!"'

'Well,' retorted Mrs. M'Cotton coldly, 'it sounded very like "The Robin's Return" to me! You crossed your hands, didn't you?'

'Only to turn the page.'

'Go on, Maisie!' urged her father. 'Play some mair! It'll make the time pass quicker till we get wur tea. Oh-oh!'

'Willie!' said Sarah, getting to her feet with sudden determination, 'I'm not going to sit here and watch you in pain like that. If you'll excuse us, Mrs. M'Cotton?'

'Oh, it's quate all right—it won't put me out in the least. Eh haven't even got the tea set yet—Eh'm depending on Jean doing it when she comes home.'

'An' when,' asked Willie feebly, 'when d'ye expect 'er?'

'Oh, any tehm after heff-pest eight.'

Willie got to his feet slowly and not without discomfort, saying with a pitiful look that only his wife understood, 'Oh, Ah think Ah'll go hame efter a', Serah. Help me. Oh!'

'Oh dear, this is terrible!' moaned Sarah. 'Peter—away you go and get the doctor. Tell him to be at our house in half an hour. Maisie—run home and put a hot bag in the bed.'

'Naw-naw!' protested Willie.

'But yes-yes!' insisted Sarah. 'Hurry, Peter!'

Peter was out of the house with an eagerness that took no account of courtesy. Maisie was about to follow him when her father laid a restraining hand on her arm:

'Don't you go, Maisie. Ye'll need tae help me.'

'Maybe we'd better to take a taxi, Willie.'

'Naw-naw,' said Willie all over again, adding that he was sure the fresh air would help him.

Mrs. M'Cotton reappeared with surprising alacrity, having

visited the newly decorated bedroom for the purpose of fetching the coats and hats of Sarah and Maisie. With further alacrity she helped Sarah into her coat while her husband helped Maisie ; Willie was left standing very still and determined to resist all offers of help should they come in his direction in the matter of a coat.

'I'm awful sorry we've spoiled your evening, Mrs. M'Cotton,' said Sarah, not paying much attention to which way her hat faced, 'but illness is illness.'

Mrs. M'Cotton waved the apology aside as a matter of no importance, while her husband had the grace to say he was sorry to see his guest in such distress. 'Where's the pain?' he queried, pawing Willie with an exploratory hand. 'Down here?'

Willie winced as he jerked away from the hand. 'Heh, don't *poke* at me!'

'Dear me, Mr. McFlehnnel,' exclaimed Mrs. M'Cotton, 'you don't need to be rude, surely!'

'Oh, you'll need to excuse him, Mrs. M'Cotton,' said Sarah, taking Willie's arm, 'he's not well. Maisie—you go to his other side. Good-night, Mr. M'Cotton. Thanks for——' she hesitated. She had been about to say 'thanks for the lovely tea' out of force of habit, but she caught herself up in time. 'Thanks for everything,' she compromised lamely.

'Good-night, Mrs. McFlannel. Good-night, Willie!' Mr. M'Cotton held out his hand as a gesture that he was willing to forgive and forget, further showing that he knew what he ought to do by asking if they were sure they wouldn't like him to come with them.

'Not at all, Jim!' came from the background of the stage from which the guests were so eager to remove themselves. 'They're better by themselves. Well, good-night. Safe home.'

'Good-night—good-night—good-night.'

The door was shut. When they were safely out of earshot and eyesight, Willie shook Maisie's hand from his arm. 'Here, you!' he said with sudden spunk, 'run efter Peter as fast as ye can. Ah don't need a doctor tae help me tae take a peen oot the tail o' ma shirt!'

Maisie was momentarily immobile from relief and surprise. Giggling raucously, she raced after her brother.

' Willie,' said Sarah reproachfully, ' is that all that was wrong with you ? Here's me worrying about—about how I'd manage —if—if I was left——'

' Ach, you ! ' Now that Willie saw prospects of amelioration he could afford to be frank. ' Hoo often have Ah tellt ye tae make sure a' the peens is oota ma new shirts ? '

' But I thought I *had* taken them all out ! '

By dint of walking with a slight crab-like motion, Willie discovered he could dodge the attentions of the pin to an extent that left his thoughts free to attend to other equally pressing matters. ' What,' he demanded, ' have ye in the hoose that ye can gi'e me fur ma tea *in a hurry* ? '

CHAPTER 12

SILVER WEDDING

HOGMANAY 1939—the twenty-fifth anniversary of Willie-and-Sarah's wedding. There was a ' phoney' war going on somewhere in France, but apart from the fact that they had to see to it that their windows were darkened thoroughly at night, it didn't affect the celebrations in any way. From early morning there was a stir about the house. For one thing there were two extra members of the family—Polly and her eight-month-old baby, now resident in Edinburgh where Dick held another and still better post with his firm. In order to let their sister and nephew have a room to themselves, Peter and Matt had shared the bed-settee in the sitting-room, and, following a night spent climbing away from each other, the two young fellows were glad to rise early to ease their aching muscles. In any case their mother wanted the room cleared in preparation for the party that was to take place later in the day.

Sarah was in a froth of excitement. ' Maisie—don't forget to see that the flowers are put in water as soon as they arrive ! ' ' Where are you, Matt ? I want you to put some red tissue paper over the hall light.' ' Peter ! How often have I to tell you not to leave towels on the bathroom floor.' ' Oh, Lassie, keep out of my road ! ' ' Maisie—see if Polly's finished with her breakfast yet.' ' Och, Willie ! None of your nonsense. I've no time for your cheepers the now ! '

And so it went on all forenoon. Polly made a belated appearance with her baby, somewhat peeved because she and her baby weren't going to be the centre of attraction in the day's proceedings. A ring at the doorbell announced the arrival of the trestle-tables and forms for the Silver Wedding tea, and for quite a while the males of the household had plenty to do to erect the contraptions. The casualties consisted of three snecked fingers, five skelfs, one crushed bunion (Willie's), a couple of inches of

133

broken wall-plaster, and ten scratches distributed impartially among the new sideboard, the piano, the bed-settee, the new oxidized kerb, and the display cabinet. Before the job was finished Sarah's face was pretty red, but the cause of that was more indirect than the other effects. And then just when Maisie was going to spread the tablecloths, it was discovered that back-smoke had got into the drawer where they had been stored and there was a black line down the folds. In exchange for being relieved of the care of her baby for an hour or two, Polly volunteered to wash, starch, and iron the tablecloths. After half an hour of Ian's restlessness, Peter began to feel he had had the worst of the bargain.

The bread-boardful of stuff from the bakery had arrived, but nothing could be done about the plates until the tablecloths were ready. There were molehills of home-made meat-shape and American tinned spiced ham ('Did Ah ever tell ye the story o' the auld chap an' the b'iled bacon? Heh, Serah, did Ah ever tell ye?'), bowls of loaf sugar, and a precious bottle of cream for the tea ; sauce bottles, pickles, beetroot. The current supply of knives was found to be inadequate, so Matt was detailed to get to work on Granny McTwill's knives with a cork and some Vim. The wedding china—or rather the remnants of it—came out, as well as the new set contributed by the family as a Silver Wedding gift ; the E.P.N.S. tea service ('Matt, you've forgotten to rub the polish off the cream jug !'), apples and oranges scrounged from all parts of the city, sweets in glass dishes ('Stop eating those chocolates, Peter ! There'll be none left for the party !'), flower-vases, plates, and saucers ('D'you not think we could risk spreading the tablecloths now, Polly?'). The windows got steamed, everybody was sweating or perspiring according to sex, a few feet ached, the heat was stifling ('Don't forget to put more coal on the sitting-room fire, Matt !'). The silver cake-basket was brought out, the cake-stand, bread-plates and more bread-plates ('Ach, we're jist in the road here ! Come on oot, Lassie ! Oot fur a walk !'), teaspoons, forks ('Watch Ian, Polly ! He's too near the table !'), still more bread-plates. . . .

By half-past six, though, the tables were set, the kitchen tidied, and one by one the family got cleaned up and dressed. Sarah had had her hair cut short for the occasion and she wasn't sure whether or not she liked it—Willie would keep drawing his hand up the back of her neck and telling her she needed a shave.

The M'Cottons, true to tradition, arrived long before the time ; on this occasion, however, there was some excuse. For one thing Mr. M'Cotton had been Willie's best man and for another they wanted to see their grandchild, and while it was a disappointment to them that their son wasn't present, Mrs. M'Cotton at any rate was convinced that his work of National Importance in Edinburgh would let everybody see how well he was getting on. When she had compared the baby unfavourably with what his father had been like at that age, she turned to Sarah and said :

' Oh, you've got your hair shingled ! Do you think it was wise ? After all, you've got a very short neck ! '

The ringing of the doorbell helped Sarah to forget the jibe. Uncle Mattha and his household had arrived with Old Auntie ; close on their heels came Aunt Polly (the bridesmaid of twenty-five years before) with her husband and family, and after that the door was just left open. It was left to Maisie to shepherd the ladies into her bedroom, while Polly and her baby shared the honours of the occasion with the bride and bridegroom. The hall was big enough to accommodate the arriving guests, though soon the crush was so intense that no-one complained of the open door. A few lucky ones occupied seats round the wall— seats that had been put out of the sitting-room to make space for the hired forms. At last everybody seemed to have arrived. Willie sought his wife in the mêlée, calling, ' Whaur's the bride ? ' With a struggle he crooked an elbow, tucked her hand into it, and was on the point of leading the way towards the sitting-room when Uncle Mattha shouted :

' Ah thocht ye sayed the beenister wis cubbid ! '

' Oh, the minister ! ' gasped Sarah. ' We can't start without him. He promised to be here. Oh—that's him now ! '

But it was a young man who stood on the doorstep—the

assistant, which was a disappointment, for the old Doctor had married them, and although they weren't great church-goers they felt that an occasion like this called for a little mild religion. Matt was ordered to look after the minister, and the procession moved, or rather pressed, forward. First Willie and Sarah, Willie with a sentimental smile on his face, Sarah not too comfortable in her new kid slippers ; then Mr. M'Cotton with Aunt Polly ; after that the members of both families in strict order of seniority—Old Auntie well in front. Mrs. M'Cotton was taken in by the minister, but it is doubtful if either of them appreciated the honour that was intended by the hosts ; fortunately for the young stranger, Matt was on his other side at the top table, and, after a rather sticky beginning following the ' Grace Before Meat,' Matt and he got on very well together. Sarah, watching the two heads together, wondered uneasily if Matt was going religious ; he was queer enough nowadays to go in for anything. There was that wee black notebook coming out again ! No, it couldn't be religion—they were both laughing too much at something Matt was reading out. What could it be ? He was a nice lad, that young minister. He was looking at Maisie. Maisie was smiling back at him—she was real tippy in that black frock. What if she and the minister. . . .

The plates were being emptied with such rapidity that it seemed as though no-one had had anything to eat that day. Maisie and Polly, pouring out tea, rushing here and there, were glad when the meal was over. They sat down at the door to listen to the speeches. They could hear Uncle Mattha deploring the fact that the toasts were being drunk in lemonade and home-made ginger-beer ' an' it Hogbaday ! ' From the bulge in his hip-pocket the girls presumed that he intended to do the toasting in his own fashion.

Mr. M'Cotton got to his feet. He was the only gentleman present—at least so his wife thought, for he was dressed in a black suit with a white shirt and a bow tie. He had got the outfit for the Staff Dance the year before and he was still rather conscious of it—a fact that perhaps explains why his speech was so stilted ; it contained so many big words, however, that it passed for a masterpiece among most of his hearers. His efforts were loudly applauded.

Willie got up to reply, and the clapping broke out afresh. ' Well, folks,' said he, placing a hand on Sarah's shoulder, ' Ah'm real gled tae be here the night. Mind ye—Ah don't know hoo Ah managed it, fur the wife here has had me deid an' buried aften anuff—whit wi' bein' run ower wi' buses an' caurs an' lorries every time Ah wis late comin' hame f'ae ma work ! ' He paused to allow similarly afflicted husbands to nudge their wives. ' But Ah'm here the night in spite o' 'er—or maybe Ah should say because o' 'er. We've had wur ups an' doons, but Ah think we've had mair ups nur doons. We're real prood tae hae wur faimly wi' us—especially Polly an' wee Ian.' The clapping broke out again in spite of the fact that several of the ladies in the company thought that Polly was giving herself far too many airs. ' There's jist one thing Ah'd like tae say—if Ah had the chance Ah wid go through it a' ower again—if Ah had the same wife ! '

The noise was deafening as he sat down ; it grew, if possible, louder as he reached forward and kissed Sarah heartily. Uncle Mattha was so rent by emotion at the spectacle that he was compelled to reach for his hankie—and the bottle wrapped in it —in his hip-pocket. After that there were speeches from Sarah's brothers and from Willie's brothers, from the young minister deputizing for his sick chief; even Uncle Mattha contributed to the oratory. What he said wasn't very coherent, but that didn't matter. He sat down with the suggestion, ' Ah thigk the bride should bake a sbeech ! '

Instantly there was a battering of knives, feet, and hands. Sarah shook her head vigorously, wondering what her genteel neighbours would be thinking about this din. Polly and Maisie from the door shouted, ' Come on, Mother ! ' and ' Don't let the men have it all their own way, Mother ! ' Willie poked at her, Matt and Peter added their coaxings, and at length she struggled to her feet, her handkerchief rolled in her moist hand like a ball. She leaned on Willie for moral support and started out bravely, carefully. Her children mustn't be ashamed of their mother.

'Ladies and gentlemen' (that was right, wasn't it?), 'it's very kind of you to say such nice things about Willie and I.' (That was good! she nearly said Willie and me.) 'It's nice that so many of the friends that were at our wedding are able to be here to-night.' (Fine. Just like the old minister's wife at the Woman's Guild.) 'We're real proud to have Polly and wee Ian here too.' (Willie had said that, though. What next? Oh, yes!) 'It's a shame that Dick couldn't get away from his work.'

There was an awkward pause. The fountain of her eloquence seemed to have dried up. She turned to look down at her husband peering up at her sideways, proudly, fondly. The sight gave her inspiration. She went on : 'We've had a real happy twenty-five years. We've been—lucky—in our family.' She stopped to look at each one individually—Matt, her favourite, queer, always far away, but strangely alive to-night ; Polly, smarter than ever, on the second rung of her own particular social ladder ; Maisie, going to fulfil her mother's ambitions at last and be a teacher—she was at the university, and Peter was going into the Tech in the New Year. It was wonderful to think that some day letters would be arriving at the house addressed to 'Miss Maisie McFlannel, M.A.' and 'Peter McFlannel, Esq., B.Sc.' Yes, they'd been lucky in their family. Sarah, still at a loss to know what to say next and still feeling she wasn't finished, groped after the thought that eluded her. She swallowed hard. She blinked—blinked again. Goodness! surely she wasn't going to cry—what was there to cry about? Some mothers might be worrying about their sons having to go to the Army or the Navy or the Air Force, but Matt was in work of National Importance at the shipyard—they couldn't take him, and Peter was too young—the war would be over long before he was eighteen. Assuredly there was nothing to cry about ; she looked back at her husband who gave her a reassuring pat on the arm. She'd got it ! She knew what she wanted to say ! It was about Willie :

'Willie was saying that he—that he—' (come on, now, what are you fumbling with your hankie for?) 'would go through it all over again if he had the same wife. Well' (oh, to hang with

speeches !), ' all Ah want tae say is—we've had many a row, an'
Ah've flyted on 'im till Ah wis black in the face, but Ah jist
want tae say the same as him—Ah'd go through it a' again—only
Ah wouldnae gi'e 'im so many rows—if Ah had the same man ! '

The success of her speech probably lay in her lapse into her
native Doric as well as in her tears ; at any rate it was generally
reckoned to be better than anybody else's. When the cheers had
died down Willie got to his feet again, saying :

' There's been toasts tae me an' Serah, an' tae the best man
an' the best maid, an' tae Auld Auntie here, an' the fam'ly an'
wee Ian, but we're no' done yet ! ' He reached down and lifted
something that had been lying at his feet. ' Here ye are ! ' he
continued, holding up Lassie for everyone to see. ' Lassie !
She's gettin' kinna white aboot the snoot, but she's gey spunky
yet. We've had 'er fur aboot twelve year noo, so she's yin o' the
fam'ly. Manys a time when there's been a collieshangie on
among the young yins, wee Lassie here has stopped it wi' sittin'
up an' beggin'. Manys a time when we've had veesitors an' we
didnae know wit tae say next, Lassie has come furrit an' done 'er
tricks.' For a moment or two Willie stroked the shaggy coat
affectionately, overcome by the thought of all she meant to him,
then he went on : ' Ah used tae think that dugs jist liked ye fur
whit ye gi'en them tae eat, but Ah've changed ma mind. Ah
think Lassie likes us fur—fur jist bein' wursels. Don't ye, pet ! '
He bent his head and the dog obediently licked his ear. ' So,
folks—drink a toast tae Lassie ! '

That part of the ceremony concluded, the tables were cleared
away, folded up, and put out on the stairhead ; the folk who had
been farthest from the fire edged nearer ; the men retired to the
kitchen for a smoke ; the ladies got together in groups to admire
Polly's baby all over again. ' Is it only nine o'clock ? ' complained Mrs. M'Cotton, who was still resentful with the young
minister for his lack of gallantry at the tea-table. A concert
followed. Maisie played the piano while Aunt Polly sang
' Bonnie wee thing ' ; Uncle Geordie recited bits of ' Tam
o' Shanter ', which didn't go down very well with some of the
ladies ; Uncle Mattha, now completely befuddled, sang a solo

unaccompanied before going quietly to sleep on one of the forms ; Polly's baby was put to bed.

Sarah, seated complacently by the fireside, looked round the company. Peter was having a fine time of it with two of his girl-cousins ; dear-dear ! conversation lozenges didn't seem to have gone out the fashion yet ! Maisie and Polly were passing round the fruit ; Willie was telling one of his funny stories to a crowd of his in-laws ; where was Matt ? My ! wasn't that like him ! Mooning away somewhere when there were visitors in the house ! This wouldn't do ! He would have to realize that a Silver Wedding was no ordinary affair. She got up and went in search of her son.

In the kitchen she found only the charwoman who had been brought in for the evening to wash the dishes. The bathroom door was standing wide open—it was just as she expected—none of the guest towels had been used, but the new turkish one was filthy. Where could Matt be ? Maisie's bedroom, cluttered with coats and hats, contained only a bevy of girls scattering face powder all over themselves and the dressing-table. Surely he wasn't in his own room ! Wee Ian was sleeping there—or ought to be ! Sarah crossed the hall and stood listening at Matt's bedroom door. The noise from the sitting-room was so great that she opened the bedroom door a fraction. T't't't ! The light was on ! Was Matt crazy ? What ! He had somebody in there with him ! She peered round the edge of the door—it was the young minister ! He was crouched in front of Matt's bookcase. Her mouth agape, Sarah's hearing was perfect as her son's words came towards her, 'Well, here it is. I hope you'll be able to make out my writing. It's pretty awful.' The young minister said, 'Thanks. I'll have a look at it, but, mind you, Editors are the best critics. Why don't you have it typed and send it to one of the local papers ?' Softly Sarah closed the door —so that was it ! More of Matt's nonsense ! Well, she couldn't very well give him a row in front of his new friend—she'd better get back to the party. What if Matt and this young man got so friendly that he came to the house a lot, would he and Maisie. . . .

Midnight was drawing near. After they'd sung *Auld Lang Syne*, Polly and Maisie would serve tea and everybody would go home. Sarah sighed with weariness—it wasn't such a thrill nowadays to stay up late as it had been twenty-five years ago. The clock climbed upwards from half-past eleven ; Uncle Mattha wakened up suddenly and asked, ' Is it Ne'erday yet ? ' Peter and his giggling cousins were playing some daft game—if they'd had this affair in the Grandiloquent as she had wanted to, they would have had some room for dancing. As it was, the room was packed to suffocation, for a lot of recent acquaintances had turned up to bring in the New Year with them. They'll go away fast enough, thought Sarah, when they find out that Willie's TT.

Two minutes to twelve ; the men looking at their watches and comparing them with the clock on the mantelpiece ; everybody getting to his feet, shuffling, ready to join hands for ' Auld Lang Syne ' ; Willie seeking her out, whispering :

' Hoo are ye, lass ? Tired ? '

' A wee bit.'

' The same here. Gi'e's yer haun'. It'll sune be ower.'

The ring was complete—over by the door were Matt and the young minister just in time to hear Maisie finishing a piano solo ; well, anyway, the minister would see that Maisie wasn't a round O. A round O ? Sarah turned the phrase over in her mind. What if Matt wasn't a round O after all ? What if he was—now what was that other phrase—oh, yes, a square peg in a round hole ? What if—what if—what if—— Ah. Twelve o'clock. ' Auld Lang Syne.' . . . ' A guid New Year tae ye ! ' ' The same to you.' ' The same to you.' ' A guid New Year.' ' The same to you an' mony o' them ! ' ' A Happy New Year, Mrs. McFlehnnel.' ' The same to you, Mrs. M'Cotton.' ' The same to you.' ' The same . . .' Lemonade. Cake. Tea. More cake. Oh, would it never end ?

One o'clock. Everybody was away, even the first-footers. If any more came they would just have to be content with seeing the young folk, for she, Sarah, was bone-tired. Willie kicked off his slippers.

'You don't mean to tell me you've been wearing these old bachles to-night?' she demanded querulously.

'Ach ay. The new yins wis geein' me jip. Ah wis in ma stockin' soles a' the time o' the tea.'

'Well I hope Mrs. M'Cotton didn't see you. You'll need to get a black suit, Willie. Jim M'Cotton looked real smart.'

'Ay-ay. Ah wis feart fur that. Ye're a great wee lass. Here—did ye mean thon?'

'Did I mean what?'

'Thon ye said aboot—aboot mairryin' the same man again?'

'Aw, Willie, don't pester me. I'm tired.'

'Ach ay, but surely it widnae hurt ye tae tell me that!'

'Well——'

'Serah, Ah've been a right turment tae ye. Ah havenae been awful accommodatin' at times, an' Ah'll never be a credit tae ye the way Jim M'Cotton is tae his wife—but—wid ye really go through the same twenty-five year again wi' me?'

Sarah looked into the dying fire, but not seeing it for the cloud of tears that dimmed her eyes. She reached out a hand sideways and Willie gripped it. 'I would that, Willie,' she said. 'All the same, manys a time it's been me that's been the torment. I've been that anxious for the young ones to get on. I couldn't help smiling at myself there—I said at the tea-table that—that I wouldn't give you so many rows—and here's me flyting on you for your slippers.'

Willie squeezed the hand that lay in his. 'Ach ay. Ye cannae help it, lass, an' Ah'd be a bonnie-like ticket withoot ye tae flyte on me. Ye're sure ye're no' feart at the idea o' maybe havin' tae spend anither twenty-five year wi' yer auld man?'

Sarah smiled. 'Not in the least. Another twenty-five years would be all right—if we were spared to one another. And—there's the family too. Right enough, Willie, we've been awful lucky with them, haven't we!'

'Ach ay, they've turned oot no' bad—conseederin'.'

'Considering what?'

'Conseederin' the wey you've worried over them. Look

hoo often in the last twenty-five year Ah've had tae tell ye tae cheer up—ye never died a winter yet ! '

Sarah made a gesture of exasperation.

' Here—come on ! ' ordered Willie.   ' Gi'e's a wee cheeper.'

He got his wee cheeper.

PRINTED IN GREAT BRITAIN AT
THE PRESS OF THE PUBLISHERS